A Time *for* Evron

BRYAN SMILLIE

Shabrya Publishing

A Time For Evron

Copyright ©(text and illustrations) 2001 by Bryan Smillie

Shabrya Publishing
P.O. Box 1171
Uxbridge, Ontario, Canada L9P 1N4
Toll free line   1-866-515-2000
Website   www.atimeforevron.com
E-mail   shabrya@sympatico.ca
Fax: 1-905-852-6287

Cover art and interior illustrations by Mike Rooth.

Cover design by Colour Innovations.

Printed and bound in Canada.

National Library of Canada Cataloguing in Publication Data
Smillie, Bryan
      A Time For Evron
ISBN 0-9689516-0-0
      I. Rooth, Mike II. Title
PS8587.M519T5 2001   jC813'.6   C2001-902584-X
PZ7.S6418T5 2001

To Arrow, R.J., and Tia.

Three of the best buds a kid could have.

ACKNOWLEDGMENTS

Many people encouraged and assisted me in producing this book. I sincerely thank:

- Cathie Petch and Megan Spafford for typing the manuscript,

- Georgia Hall and Ryan Spafford for editorial work,

- Mike Rooth for his brilliant rendering of my ideas into illustrations,

- Rosemarie Gawelko at Warner Bros. Publications and Kevin Richards at SONY/ATV for permission to quote "BELIEVE IN YOU",

- Marsha Whelan, Executive Director of the Network of Sacred Heart Schools in Boston, for permission to quote the excerpt from "Life at the Sacred Heart",

- Mom and Dad, Audrey and Don Smillie, the best parents a kid could have,

- And finally, but most importantly, my wife, Shannon, for her unwavering support for this and all my other projects.

PROLOGUE

MATTHEW WAS SITTING QUIETLY ON HIS BED, staring at his new class picture. These pictures always came out near the middle of June, just before school ended for the summer holidays. His teacher, Mr. Sobalsky, had said that they were a sort of pictorial time capsule because they captured a split second in time when all the people were there in one group, a moment when they were all together as one. It would probably never happen again.

Matt slowly studied each face. Some of the images made him smile wistfully, thinking of happy times with these people, and the fun they had shared together. Other faces made him think of the new experiences which they had added to his life. They were new friends and they had brought with them all that was part of their lives. He looked at Nadja and thought of how he never would have believed he could fall so madly for one girl.

As his eyes slowly swept over the three rows of faces, their eyes were quiet as they looked back from the picture. There was no laughter, nor tears, nor anger, nor excitement emanating from the glossy photo's surface. No one would ever know from the picture the stories in their lives.

There were so many memories of the experiences he had shared with the other kids and of the moments when he and just one or two of his friends shared a secret, a thought, or an emotion. Most often no one else knew, or would ever know, about those past times together.

Evron, of course, knew a lot of the time what was going on in all their lives. He had been such a great help to so many of the kids in the past year. What would they ever have done without him? Matt had thought at the time that Evron should be in the class picture too, but then realized how silly it would be to have a dog sitting there in the school photograph. And why just one dog? No one would ever believe that he was a talking dog from another galaxy in space. No one would believe that he had arrived on Earth to help its kids with problems in their day-to-day lives, or how he had helped Matthew and his friends so many times. No one would ever believe it.

Matthew laughed to himself, thinking of the times Mr. Sobalsky would pause while teaching and look out from their second floor class window and comment on the hundreds of roof tops he saw surrounding the school. He would say to his students, "Just think for a moment of all the thousands of lives that are going on under those roofs. Think of the thousands of mothers, fathers, grandparents, brothers and sisters who live in this one small neighborhood alone. Think of all the emotions that are going on in their lives every day."

Matthew was thinking now of how his life and the lives of his friends must, at times, look so great to others. He was thinking of how often he had heard from adults how they wished they were kids again when life was so simple and carefree. He wished that they realized how difficult at times it was for kids, and how their lives could be just as complicated as an adult's.

He knew deep down that his mom and dad, his teachers, and most adults cared a lot about kids. He knew they wanted to help out young people like himself as much as they could. But, there were times when kids just didn't want to share their thoughts and problems with adults. Sometimes kids just didn't want to, or couldn't, talk about their problems, even with their own friends.

This is why Evron had been so great. He was the one friend they could all talk to. If only every kid could have an Evron!

And so this is the story. It involves a young boy, Matthew, and his talking dog, Evron.

Evron, along with eleven of his dog friends, came to Earth from another planet far away in space. They travelled here to see how Earth's young people would respond to them. On Evron's planet, the animals and the kids talk to each other. The dogs are confidantes to the young people and the kids can talk to them about their problems, their fears, and their private feelings. When they cannot relate to their parents or teachers or friends, they can always talk to their friend Evron in privacy and confidentiality.

Evron is mature and caring, like a wise old sage. In this novel, he helps Matthew and his friends through their personal difficulties and in their day-to-day interactions with others. Whether they are experiencing first love, anger, fear, death, jealousy, hurt, or a host of other emotions, Evron is there to guide them. Sometimes he gives direct advice; at other times, he helps them work out the decisions on their own.

This is a novel about young people growing up and dealing with life's everyday challenges.

Everyone needs an Evron by his or her side to help out.

CONTENTS

PROLOGUE v

"BELIEVE IN YOU"...x

INTRODUCTION 1

CHAPTER 1 - THE BIRTHDAY PRESENT 3

CHAPTER 2 - THE DREAM 7

CHAPTER 3 - A SECOND FRIEND 11

CHAPTER 4 - SPRING FEVER 15

CHAPTER 5 - THE CANOE TRIP 21

CHAPTER 6 - THE RESCUE..27

CHAPTER 7 - LETTING GO 33

CHAPTER 8 - PUPPY LOVE 37

CHAPTER 9 - TESTING FRIENDSHIPS...................................43

CHAPTER 10 - A NEW FRIEND 49

CHAPTER 11 - MORE PROBLEMS 55

CHAPTER 12 - FISHY BUSINESS 63

CHAPTER 13 - BAD GIRLS...73

CHAPTER 14 - A WAR HERO..83

CHAPTER 15 - A GUEST TEACHER 91

CHAPTER 16 - BASKETBALL FEVER.....................................99

CHAPTER 17 - A NEW NEIGHBOR.......................................109

CHAPTER 18 - SEPARATION AND LOSS 121

CHAPTER 19 - WORLDWIDE TERROR 129

CHAPTER 20 - MONEY PROBLEMS 137

CHAPTER 21 - THE SLEEPOVER 145

CHAPTER 22 - A FEELING OF SELF-WORTH 151

CHAPTER 23 - SPECIAL POWER 163

CHAPTER 24 - HURTING OTHERS.......................................171

CHAPTER 25 - MORE THAN JUST A FRIEND 179

CHAPTER 26 - MOVING ON 183

AUTHOR'S LETTER 188

"BELIEVE IN YOU"*

"Somewhere someone's reaching
Trying to grab that ring
Somewhere there's a silent voice
Learning how to sing
Some of us can't move ahead
We're paralyzed with fear
And everybody's listening
'Cause we all need to hear

I believe in you
I can't even count the ways that
I believe in you
And all I want to do is help you to
Believe in you
I will hold you up
I will help you stand
I will comfort you when you need a friend
I will be the voice that's calling out
I believe in you"

INTRODUCTION

THERE WERE MANY UFO SIGHTINGS on Earth that autumn. They were occurring everywhere. Even in Russia, people claimed to have seen a strange unidentified flying object land, and peculiar looking little creatures disembark. They were hard to describe though, because it was dark then and they were too far away.

One farmer in the U.S.A. took experts to one of his fields where he said a large UFO had crushed his hay. No one else had seen it, however, and no one could explain how it got there.

There were many sightings in the sky as well, usually at night. Fast moving and spinning lights were seen going in many directions. Even when people took pictures or videos, it was still hard to understand exactly what they were looking at.

From all the sightings, however, there were two things that were fairly certain: the creatures inside these UFO's were probably visiting from outer space, and they were not dangerous because no one had ever been harmed by them. Beyond this, no one knew anything about them.

One dog was especially affectionate; he immediately licked Matt's face and snuggled closely into his arms.

CHAPTER ONE

THE BIRTHDAY PRESENT

AS HE WOKE up early that Saturday morning, Matthew was very excited. It was his birthday, the day he had been awaiting for a long time. The extra special thing about this birthday was that he was finally going to get a dog. He had thought about this dog for weeks, and all the possible sizes, shapes, and colors from which he could choose.

His dad was going to take him to the local animal shelter that morning. Matt was going to choose a dog from several litters of young pups. His heart raced at the thought of it all. He would be able to bring the dog home today so that everyone could see it at his party that night.

This was an extra special day for him for another reason too; his mom and younger sister, Amy, were coming to the party. Since his mom and dad had divorced last year, things had been really difficult for Matthew. He was sad a lot because he missed them so much since they had left to live in another town. Although Amy sometimes visited for weekends, his mother had never been back.

The past year hadn't been fun for anyone in the family. At first, Matthew had not understood what was happening. Although his parents argued a lot, he was shocked when his mother decided to leave. She wanted to take both Amy and Matthew with her, but his dad thought each parent should keep one child. Matt was upset because he loved both parents. He wanted to stay with both, but how could he?

It had been a tough time. He had cried a lot, and he was not doing well at school. He just wasn't as happy as he used to be. He wanted everything back the way it was before.

But he was feeling good this morning. The only thing on his mind was his dog. Matt rushed his father through breakfast and they were soon on their way to the kennel.

"How much further, Dad?" he asked excitedly.

"About five more minutes," his father replied calmly, trying to settle him down.

Finally they arrived. As they entered the main kennel area, Matthew's mouth dropped. All he could see were rows and rows of cages. It seemed as if hundreds of dogs were whining and barking all at once.

"Follow me please," said the kennel attendant; "I'll take you to the young puppy area."

One of the cages there contained six pups about ten weeks old. Each one was light brown in colour. They all rushed to the cage door as Matt leaned over to look more closely. They were all so cute and cuddly.

"Dad, how will I choose?" Matt asked, worriedly.

"Why not take out each one and cuddle it for a few minutes? Maybe that will help you decide," replied his father.

Matt thought that was a good idea; so did the kennel attendant.

One dog was especially affectionate; he immediately licked Matt's face and snuggled closely into his arms.

"I'm going to take this one," Matt said happily as he smiled at the kennel attendant. His dad thought this was a good choice too.

On the way home in the car, the puppy lay curled up in Matt's lap. He seemed happy to have a human body close to him.

A Time for Evron

"Have you thought of a name for him yet?" Matt's father asked.

"No, not really. I've thought of lots of names, but I haven't found one I really like. Maybe tonight I'll think of one."

When they arrived home, Matt had the pup's bed, and food and water bowls all ready for him. The new family member was going to stay in the kitchen for a while until he was paper trained and familiar with his new home. In the meantime, Matt had to help his father get ready for his party.

Later that afternoon, many of Matt's friends came to the party, and he received some really special presents. Dad barbecued hot dogs and everyone played games in their big backyard. The cake his mom baked was really good too. Having his mom and Amy back home for the day had been really wonderful just like it used to be. As evening settled in, his friends gradually left for their homes.

Matt hadn't been happier in months. But now it was time for his mom and Amy to leave. Kissing his mom and Amy good bye was very difficult for Matt. He had a big lump in his throat, as he watched them drive away. He and his father didn't say much as they cleaned up the party dishes. Matt thought his father was sad too.

As Matt dried his eyes and rolled over, he felt a small furry body snuggle closely to him.

CHAPTER TWO

THE DREAM

THAT FIRST NIGHT HOME WITH HIS NEW PUPPY was a difficult one for Matthew. Every time the pup scratched the kitchen door or whimpered, Matt woke up and went to see him. He wasn't getting much sleep. Finally he brought the small dog into his bedroom with him. Everything seemed fine as he turned out the lights and fell quickly into a deep sleep.

When he next woke up, it was still the middle of the night. Matthew had tears in his eyes and had been crying a lot; his pillow was wet.

He had been dreaming that he was pleading with his mom and sister not to leave him after his party. They had been crying too. "Please don't go; please stay with Dad and me!" he cried.

"We have to go dear," his mother replied. "Things just won't work out anymore between your dad and me."

As Matt dried his eyes and rolled over, he felt a small furry body snuggle closely to him. He was frightened at first and pulled back quickly. When he turned on his bed-side light, he saw that his new puppy was in bed with him.

The dog spoke very softly, "Hello Matthew, my name is Evron."

Matthew could hardly believe his eyes and ears.

Evron continued, "I am here to be your friend and to help you. I understand why you're crying about your mom and sister." Matt couldn't quite believe it, but his new dog was actually talking to him!

He replied, "I don't want Dad to know I cry about it; it will only upset him."

"That is why I can help you," explained Evron. "You can talk to me instead."

Matt started to feel better as Evron continued. "Sometimes, it's better for mothers and fathers not to be together anymore when they don't get along. They're happier separated."

Matt and Evron talked about how Matt felt for over two hours. As he discussed his feelings with Evron, Matt began to understand that his family could never again be the way it was before. As Evron said, "Sometimes you have to accept things as they are, if you can't change them. You can still see and love your mom and Amy, but your home situation will be different. Time won't heal all your pain, Matthew, but it will hurt less with time."

Matthew nodded thoughtfully. "You're right, Evron. They're still my family; that won't change. And at least Amy and I don't have to listen to them arguing anymore."

"But Evron," he continued, "who are you and how did you get into that dog kennel?"

The sun was just starting to come up as Evron began to tell his life story. He was born on another planet, millions of kilometers away in space. On his planet, kids and animals were close and equal friends. They lived together and played together like some on Earth, but there was a much deeper bond. They often talked about things that kids felt they could not discuss with their parents.

"On my planet, Matthew, we are true confidantes," Evron said. "We exchange secrets and private feelings with each other. A short while ago, some other dogs and I decided to travel to Earth. We want to try and help some of you as well."

Matthew thought this was a great idea. "How many more like

you are here on earth, Evron?" he asked.

"Twelve of us came on this trip, Matthew. We've landed in several countries, all over the world. We usually arrive at night so that we're not easily seen; then we sneak into kennels to pose as normal animals."

"Hoping someone like me will come and pick you up," laughed Matt.

"That's the idea," smiled Evron.

"Now I don't have to pick a name for you, but Dad will wonder how in the world I ever thought of the word 'Evron'," Matt chuckled.

Evron continued, "Our purpose right now, Matthew, is to see how young people like yourself respond to us. We want to help you. We want to teach you not only to think for yourselves, but also to help others."

"You mean like you've already helped me with my feelings about Mom and Dad's divorce?" asked Matthew.

"That's right," replied Evron.

Matthew loved listening to Evron. "I can hardly wait for school on Monday so I can tell all my friends about you!"

"Not so fast!" replied Evron. "Let's work slowly and talk to only one friend at a time. First of all, Matthew, I want you to listen to a friend's problem by yourself. If you have trouble helping him or her, then I will give you some assistance."

Matthew thought for a moment, then said, "I know just the friend, Evron. He is very unhappy right now and I'm going to try and help him. His name is Carlo."

The next day Evron met with Carlo. At first, Carlo's mouth fell open in disbelief and he said to Matthew, "You're playing games with me. This can't be a real live dog talking to me!"

CHAPTER THREE

A SECOND FRIEND

CARLO HAD BEEN VERY UPSET FOR A LONG TIME because he could not play on the school's football team. He was an excellent athlete and had easily made the team tryouts. His problem was that he did not have enough money for the team equipment.

The school was willing to help him with the expenses, but his parents would not let him ask his teacher. They were proud people who were recent immigrants to the country. They were beginning a new life here and could not afford to spend money on the team gear and uniform.

"We have more important things to do with our money," said Carlo's father.

Matthew and Carlo talked for a long time that afternoon. Matthew listened carefully to his friend's problem, but could not seem to help him, or to make him feel any better. Carlo finally said, "My father is very set in his ways, Matthew. There is no changing his mind and he won't allow any further discussion about it. My mom tried to talk to him too. He just won't listen anymore."

When Matthew saw Evron later that day, he was very worried. "Nothing I say to Carlo seems to help. He's still very upset." Evron agreed to sit down and talk with both of them.

The next day Evron met with Carlo. At first, Carlo's mouth fell open in disbelief and he said to Matthew, "You're playing games with me. This can't be a real live dog talking to me!"

He soon recovered from his shock though, and listening to Evron, he discovered some things he had not thought about before. He was good in all sports, not just in football. If he could not play this game, then why not try some others?

Evron said, "Why don't you concentrate on track and field?"

"There is no track until next spring," Carlo responded.

"That may be so," replied Evron, "but you can train in the school all winter and be ready for the tryouts in the spring. It won't be necessary to buy expensive equipment either. All you really need is your own determination and skill."

Carlo thought this was a good idea. "You're right, Evron; if I can't play football, then I should try to do my best in some other activity. Why worry about things I can't change? All I really need for track and field is a good pair of running shoes and some track shorts. And I already have both."

Matt was listening to them both carefully. They were getting along beautifully. He thought to himself, "In many ways, Evron's advice to Carlo was the same as it is for me. It's only the situations that are different."

"Thanks for helping, Carlo," Matthew said. "I only wish I had thought of that myself."

"Yeah Matthew, why didn't you think of that?" Carlo chuckled.

Evron smiled and said, "Don't worry. Thinking problems through like this doesn't always come easily. It takes practice and experience. You're both very young. That's why I'm here to help you."

Evron had a warm feeling inside. Both boys were feeling much better about themselves since he had arrived. It seemed the young earth beings enjoyed having him as their new friend.

A Time for Evron

As time went by and group members got to know each other better, Matthew discovered a lot about Marsha.

CHAPTER FOUR

SPRING FEVER

THE WINTER TERM at school passed by quickly that year. Everyone seemed delighted that the snow and ice had finally melted, and that the days were getting warmer and longer. Matt said to Evron and Carlo one day, "It's funny how you get excited about spring after a cold winter. There's something special about riding your bike again for the first time."

Evron, Matthew and Carlo had become close friends. Because no one knew their secret, the three appeared perfectly normal to others.

Matthew's football team had lost out in the semi-final matches that season, but Carlo had recently won most of his events in track and field. He had trained hard all winter and his great conditioning had finally paid off. He was voted the top male athlete for his class. Evron was sure Carlo wouldn't have done as well in track and field if he had spent all his time on football instead. "It's funny how sometimes things turn out for the best, isn't it?" he said with a big grin. Matt and Carlo understood what he meant.

As the warmer days of summer approached, and the school term was winding down, all attention turned to the most exciting event of the school year – the annual canoe trip. Everyone in the class went along. There were no tryouts and no competition involved. Teachers helped with paddling instructions, back-packing techniques, and outdoor survival skills. Everyone worked together for weeks to make the trip a big success.

Matthew was really excited when he was elected by the class as one of the team captains. There were four teams of canoeists with six students on each team.

Matthew felt lucky when he was allowed to pick Carlo as his assistant captain. That evening after school, the captains had to meet in private to choose other class members for their teams. There had to be an equal number of girls and boys on each team.

That night Matthew and Carlo reviewed the class names in order to decide whom to choose. They laughed as they discussed the various girls they would like on their team.

"Let's put Rachael on our team," said Carlo. "I think she's really cute and she's smart too."

"Okay," replied Matthew, "but certainly not Marsha."

"You're right; no way for her," laughed Carlo. "No one likes her anyway. Besides she punched Jason the other day when he called her 'tubby'."

Marsha was not popular in the class. She had moved from another school that year and no one knew much about her. Because she was overweight and wore glasses, some of the other kids teased her. She didn't talk much and didn't seem very friendly.

Carlo continued. "She will probably be a bad influence on whatever team she's on. Let's avoid her if we can."

Matt agreed. "Let's choose someone else. Hopefully another team will pick Marsha."

Evron was lying quietly on the floor as the boys talked. For a

A Time for Evron

short while, they had forgotten about him and had not included him in the discussion. Evron shocked them as he spoke. "I think you should choose Marsha," he said. Both boys stared at him.

"Why would we choose her if we don't have to?" Carlo asked.

"Maybe she seems unfriendly because no one has ever tried really talking to her," Evron replied. "Besides, if someone made fun of you two for some reason, you wouldn't be exactly friendly either."

Both boys sat quietly, thinking about what Evron was saying.

"Don't judge people just by the way they look," he continued. "Perhaps if you take the time to get to know Marsha, you might even like her."

"But we don't have much time," replied Carlo.

Their first reaction was to forget about Evron's advice. They discussed it further, however, and realized he was probably right. Matt said, "I guess we should really try to put ourselves in her shoes. Why not give her a chance?"

Both boys had faced their own problems. They thought about this and how their new friend Evron had helped them work these out. They also remembered what he had told them earlier about learning not only to help themselves, but also to help others as well.

The next day, on their way to school, Carlo told Matt he had an even better idea about Marsha. "Why not make Marsha the assistant captain of the team instead of me? I'm popular anyway and will be picked up quickly by one of the other groups."

"Great idea," replied Matt. "I wish I had thought of it first."

"Maybe next time," laughed Carlo.

This was an even better idea than Evron's advice yesterday. They knew he would be proud of them.

When Matthew's choice of Marsha as his new assistant captain was announced at school, the class was shocked. No one said much, but many students were obviously confused. Matt just kept smiling as the captains and assistant captains were excused to go to the library in order to divide the class into teams.

As they left the room together, Marsha said, "Thanks, Matthew, for choosing me, but I don't understand why."

Matt smiled at her and said, "I needed some girls on my team anyway and because you're new to the school, Carlo and I thought it would be a good way to make you feel more welcome."

"So Carlo was involved in this decision too?"

"Sure!" responded Matt, grinning. "Great minds think alike."

Marsha was grateful. She had been frightened about being on a team with people she didn't know. Matthew was making her feel better already.

Once all the teams were selected, everyone met for an hour each day with their teacher advisors to prepare for the trip. They discussed such things as proper paddling techniques, outdoor survival skills, and the best kinds of food and clothing to take for a couple of days and nights in the wilderness. As time went by, and group members got to know each other better, Matthew discovered a lot about Marsha. She had won several awards in swimming at her last school. Her best time was in the butterfly stroke where she had set a new school record. Unlike most students her age, Marsha had done a lot of canoeing. Her family loved the outdoors and they often went hiking and back-packing on weekends. Last year, on her dad's holidays, they even tried some mountain climbing.

A Time for Evron

Matthew was amazed to discover these things about Marsha. He realized appearances were deceiving. Evron was right - no one had really given Marsha a chance to talk about herself.

Everything was going well until halfway across the lake.

CHAPTER FIVE

THE CANOE TRIP

THE WEEK OF THE CANOE TRIP FINALLY ARRIVED and the first day and night in the woods had gone well. The weather was warm, the bugs were not too bad, and everybody was over the jitters of being in their own canoes. The teachers organized the tents at the camp the first night and Matthew's team was in charge of the first cookout. Everyone sang campfire songs and told ghost stories late into the night.

There had been one last minute surprise addition to the trip: Evron.

Evron had asked Matt, "Please ask your teacher if I can come along. It would be a great experience for me to be with all the other students and to get more involved with your young friends." Matthew's teacher had finally agreed to include Evron. The class was excited. They thought he would be a great school mascot.

The second morning of the trip started out mild and breezy. After an early breakfast and camp clean-up, everybody was ready to put their canoes in the water. There was only one note of concern now - the winds which were getting stronger and blowing out of the northwest.

The first part of their trip that morning was going to take them across a large open part of the lake. They were concerned that the winds would blow them off course. If they canoed around the far shore though, it would take them an extra day to arrive at their pick-up point. Because they were imitating the explorers of hundreds of years earlier, no cell phones or other modern day equipment was allowed on the trip. Therefore, no one would know where they were and their parents would be worried. They decided to cross the middle of the lake, canoeing directly into the wind.

Everything was going well until the canoes were halfway across the lake. The winds were stronger now and the waves were getting higher. The students were getting tired with the heavy paddling. Suddenly Matthew's lead canoe swung around sideways. As it swung around, it was hit by a large wave and flipped over like a small toy boat. The kids and their camping gear were thrown into the cold water. Matt, Evron, and two other team members were being tossed about in the high waves.

Marsha and the rest of her team were in the second canoe. She was struggling too, and barely heard Matthew as he called into the wind. As she turned toward his voice, she gasped in horror at what she saw. She looked quickly around the lake for all the remaining campers.

By this time, unfortunately, all eight canoes were in trouble. They were all being blown around and now another one had overturned into the frigid waters. In the meantime, Matthew had grabbed Evron and was trying to swim towards Marsha. She was paddling frantically in his direction, screaming instructions to the others with her. As they approached, Matt eased Evron into the canoe with one big push. Marsha leaned over to grab Matthew as the wind blew them by. Stripping off her lifejacket, she threw it to him for added buoyancy. She missed him and he was soon out of reach.

Marsha had two other team members with her: Connie and Ajay. Both were sobbing and frantically holding onto the sides of the canoe. They were terrified that it was going to tip like the others.

A Time for Evron

"What are we going to do, what are we going to do?" Connie screamed.

"Just sit there and try to settle down," Marsha replied. She too was frightened and was trying to control the canoe by herself now. Once in the canoe, Evron shook himself dry and was sitting up looking directly at Marsha. "Don't try to fight the winds," he said gently. "Instead, steer with them to that nearest shore over there."

Naturally Marsha couldn't believe her ears. She stared at him in stunned silence; then she choked out, "Wha ... What?"

"Steer for that shoreline," Evron repeated, pointing over her shoulder to the nearest point of land.

She looked back quickly to check the distance. "But there's a small island not too far ahead."

"We'll never make it," Evron replied. "The winds are too strong."

"But what about the others?"

"Just try to get to land first; then we can go for help."

Marsha turned the canoe toward the shoreline. Evron was impressed with her paddling ability, considering she had to do it all by herself since Connie and Ajay were still too frightened to move. As they approached shore, the canoe bottom scraped and cracked as it slid onto the rocks.

"Oh my gosh," groaned Marsha; "we've wrecked the canoe!"

"Don't worry about that now," yelled Evron. "Let's get our supplies out before it sinks."

The canoe did sink slowly into the frigid lake. Fortunately, the team members were all safe on land. They squinted into the winds as they looked for the others on the lake. They could see no one. Everything was quiet for a moment, then Connie cried, "No one will ever find us here. Where are the others?"

"They're probably safe on land too. Don't worry; we'll be alright," Marsha tried to reassure her.

She was terrified as well, but was determined to put on a good front in order to keep the others calm. Marsha hoped that some of the outdoor camping lessons she had learned with her father would help her now.

"We'd better get a fire started so that we can keep warm," she continued. "We also have to build a lean-to for shelter because our tent was in Matt's canoe."

"Oh no!" moaned Ajay.

"Don't worry; just help me build it. I'll show you how," she said, hoping she could remember her father's instructions from past trips.

Evron had been quiet since they had reached shore. Marsha knew he was watching and listening to her though. She wanted to talk to him, but not in front of Ajay and Connie. They were finally calming down and she didn't want to upset them again by seeing her talking to a dog.

Once the fire was started, and their lean-to erected, Marsha said, "I'm going to get more firewood now. Evron can come with me; we'll be back in about five minutes."

Once they were both out of sight, Marsha said, "Evron, who are you really?" He told her to sit down for a minute and explained again the story that only Matt and Carlo knew. She wasn't as surprised as they had been.

"I've always felt there was other life somewhere in space," she said. "I'm glad you're here with me Evron; I'm not as scared now."

"You're doing very well indeed, Marsha. Carlo and Matthew made a wise choice when they selected you." She smiled back as he winked at her.

"But what do you think we should do now?" she asked.

"I think you and I should try to make it out of the woods and go for help. Ajay and Connie will be safe here."

"What about Matthew and the others?"

"We can't be sure, of course, but there were islands nearby. Maybe they reached one. We can't assume anything though. I'm afraid we're on our own."

Marsha was staring ahead into the warm campfire. She was in deep thought as her head rested wearily on her folded arms.

CHAPTER SIX

THE RESCUE

AFTER EXPLAINING THE PLAN to Ajay and Connie, Marsha and Evron trekked off alone into the forest. Marsha was really happy he was with her.

"Don't worry, Marsha; we'll find help," Evron said encouragingly.

The winds were getting worse now and it was starting to rain. They had walked for almost three hours as darkness started to fall. Hoping to find a major highway, they had been heading south. They marked their trail as they traveled and Marsha's skill in the woods kept them moving in the right direction. They knew they were not going in circles. Evron was impressed with her knowledge of the outdoors and her ability to take care of herself. With his encouragement, she was doing fine.

In a tired voice, Marsha finally said, "Let's make camp now, Evron. We're starting to get really wet. We can rest awhile and dry by a fire."

Evron agreed. "We can start again early in the morning."

As they crouched by the fire that night, the rain sprinkled lightly on the cedar boughs of their lean-to. The flames were hypnotizing as they flickered quietly among the pieces of firewood. Marsha was in a talkative mood. She was growing fond of her new canine friend and felt she could trust him with her feelings.

"Evron," she murmured, "do you mind if I ask you a question?"

"Of course not," he replied, wondering what Marsha would ask him.

"Do you like me?"

Evron was shocked. "Of course I do, Marsha; why wouldn't I?"

"I just wondered. I'm curious."

Evron replied, "I think you've done really well with all of the problems we've had on this trip. You've kept calm and you're doing a great job of leading us out of here. Don't worry; we will find somebody to help us tomorrow."

"Oh, I don't mean that way, Evron. I mean, do you like the way I look and everything?"

"What's wrong with the way you look, Marsha?"

"Well, I'm really too fat for my age, Evron, and I hate wearing these glasses. I want to look like the girls I see on T.V., and in the movies and magazines."

Evron sat quietly for a moment. "Don't forget Marsha that the image makers in the media are often trying to show people a level they feel is perfection. Many times, those young women are not accurate portrayals of real life."

"Oh, I know a lot of it is for show, but it's really hard when you're my age not to want to look as pretty as they are."

"I understand," he replied. "Of course you want to feel good about how you look. Everyone does – even adults. But don't forget; we're all unique. Everyone's size and shape is different. Remember, too, that girls your age are in or near puberty and are undergoing body changes beyond their control. I think you call this process 'hormones' here on Earth."

Marsha was staring ahead into the warm campfire. She was in deep thought as her head rested wearily on her folded arms. Then she sighed, "Oh yes, 'hormones,' there's always someone talking about 'hormones'. I guess what you're saying is it's good to care about all this stuff to a point, but we shouldn't beat ourselves up over it."

"Maybe you should be a little bit easier on yourself, Marsha," Evron continued.

Marsha perked up a bit. "Obviously, I should be cutting back on a lot of the junk food I eat. That would sure help. And when I'm swimming and competing in the pool, I feel really good about myself. I'm going to try and concentrate more on the positive." Evron nodded approvingly.

"But what about my glasses?" she blurted out. "Too much junk food didn't make my eyesight bad. I really would like to get contact lenses but my parents say that's a luxury they can't afford right now."

"Why not pay for them yourself?" Evron shot back.

"Myself? Where would I get the money?"

"Let's look at the possibilities," he continued. "What are some things you could do?"

"I babysit occasionally. I've saved some money from that, but not a whole lot."

"What do you spend your babysitting money on?"

"Well, yeah, I do spend some of it on things I don't need like chocolate and chips. I could save that way. I probably buy too many C.D.'s at times too. I'm sort of an impulse buyer."

Evron was smiling at Marsha now. "So I guess part of your plan to get contact lenses will consist of establishing some priorities."

"How do you mean?"

"Well, if you decide you really want them, you can give up certain things to save money for the lenses."

"Yeah, I really want them badly, Evron. Maybe I can get another job as well. I saw an ad in the paper for newspaper carriers. Do you think I should apply?"

"What do you think you should do?"

"Why not?" she replied quickly, sounding more determined than ever. "I'm going to fill out an application as soon as I get home. And besides, delivering newspapers will be good exercise for me."

They both sat quietly for a few minutes watching the fire. Its warm glow was comforting on this otherwise cold, damp evening. Finally Marsha broke the long silence. "Evron, thanks for listening and helping me help myself. I've never really talked to anyone like this before, about this personal stuff. It's nice to have someone like you there for me. I'm determined to change some things in my life."

Then Evron snuggled up to her arm, and Marsha hugged him as the rain came down harder. As their roof began to leak, she realized that, before she made any changes in her life, she had to get them out of this mess.

A Time for Evron

*Two days later, a special funeral service was held at the school.
An overflow crowd filled the auditorium and halls. Following the
service, Marsha and Matthew walked home together in tears.*

CHAPTER SEVEN

LETTING GO

THE NEXT COUPLE OF DAYS were very sad ones for everyone. They began with relief and excitement for Marsha when she and Evron finally found a highway and flagged down a passing motorist for help. Marsha was a heroine. The girl no one knew very well or liked very much at first, was now leading rescuers to the stranded campers.

The rescuers had terrible news though. Three boys had died in the icy waters the day before. Carlo had been one of them. Even though all the boys were wearing life jackets, they couldn't survive in the cold waters of the lake. Despite the fact that the weather had been warm, the lakes still hadn't heated up after the previous extremely cold winter. The horrible news made headlines on radio and TV all over the country.

Two days later, a special funeral service was held at the school. An overflow crowd filled the auditorium and halls. Following the service, Marsha and Matthew walked home together in tears. They were talking about Carlo. Matthew was crying because he had lost an old friend; Marsha was crying because she had lost a new one. As they approached Matthew's front yard, Evron was waiting for them; they ran over and cuddled him.

Matthew had tears in his eyes as he said, "How could this happen Evron? Why did Carlo have to die?"

Evron was quiet and thought for a long time before he spoke. "I don't know, Matthew. Even on my planet, we have no answers to explain the mysteries of life and death. Although we're more advanced than earthlings, we're still uncertain about many things." He paused to wipe tears from his own eyes. "Just remember this," he said; "Carlo was your friend and you loved him. Even though he's gone now, the things that you loved about him will comfort you and memories of him will always be with you. Because life is so fragile and can be lost so quickly, we must learn to live to the fullest everyday. We must care for all creatures, whether human or animal. One of the reasons I have visited you here on Earth is to help you understand this idea."

Marsha and Matthew were sitting quietly on the front porch as Evron spoke. Both stared ahead, lost in a daze of their own private thoughts, while listening to his words. It would take a long time before any of them began to feel normal again.

A Time for Evron

*One afternoon, while he was lazily eating an ice cream cone
and watching everyone swimming, suddenly a beachball
flew over the pool fence in his direction.*

CHAPTER EIGHT

PUPPY LOVE

THE TRAGIC DEATHS HAD OCCURRED near the end of the school year. This was normally a happy time for all school kids, but, of course, this year was very different. The few remaining weeks of the school term went by very slowly, and everyone was generally very quiet and sad.

The last day of school brought no 'hoots and hollers' as it normally would have done. Instead, as the last bell rang, everybody sadly said their good-byes and went off for their summer vacations.

One new development for Matt was his dad's new job. He had taken over as the manager of a gasoline station and variety store just outside town. Matt liked his dad's new job because now he could see more of his father, and he found it exciting to be around all the hustle and bustle of the gas station. It also helped him to keep busy and not to dwell on Carlo's death.

There were still occasions, though, when Matthew missed his friend a lot. But to his own surprise, there were also times when he was happy again, or even when he laughed. Then he felt badly because he had, for a short time, forgotten his friend. He wondered how he could be happy again like this without Carlo.

He remembered Evron's words, however. "Life goes on and

you'll always have a special place in your heart for those you love". He knew that Carlo would want him to carry on without him.

As the summer days rolled slowly by, and Matthew spent long hours at the service station just hanging around, he decided to ask his father if he could get a job there.

His father's reply had been swift and direct: "No." He simply felt that Matt was too young to work at a gas station, and the summer holidays were a time for kids to play and have fun.

Matt was very disappointed, and sadly told Evron about his dad's response that night. He grinned broadly when Evron said, "I agree with you that you should have a job and it's good for you to learn some responsibility and to learn about commitment. It also helps you to work with others and to learn about the world outside of school and play". With Evron's quiet support, Matt persisted with his father to give him some jobs to do. He was too young to operate the cash register or to pump the gasoline, but his father finally gave in and allowed Matt to help out in other ways.

Some of Matthew's jobs were to keep the store floor clean, to make coffee for the customers, and to empty the garbage cans near the gasoline pumps. Sometimes he cleaned car windshields if the cars were small enough. He really liked these jobs because he got to meet lots of customers. Most people were nice to him, but some others were grumpy. He was learning to deal with all types of people. He was really happy to be helping out his dad and he was putting the small amount of money he made each day into his savings account at the nearby bank.

The service station was near a busy highway interchange. It was surrounded by restaurants and motels for the many travelers and commuters passing through the area. Just beside their gas station was a popular motel with a swimming pool. Although the pool was only for motel guests, Matthew often walked by it on his break to watch everyone swimming and splashing about. It was turning out to be a hot summer vacation and he wished he could go swimming there as well.

One afternoon, while he was lazily eating an ice cream cone and watching everyone swimming, a beachball suddenly flew over the pool fence in his direction. Matt ran and caught it to the cheers of those in the pool. As he approached the fence to throw it over, he noticed a young girl about his age with her arms outstretched. She caught his return throw and then came up to Matthew. "Thank you... my name is Jessica. What's yours?"

"Hi, I'm Matthew." He could hardly get the words out because Jessica had to be the cutest girl he had ever seen in his life and he instantly became very shy.

"Why don't you come in swimming with us?" she yelled over the screaming and laughter of the other swimmers.

"Only guests of the motel can swim here," replied Matthew.

"I think friends of guests can swim too; I'll ask Mom," Jessica said as she dashed to the far side of the pool.

Matthew was still in shock that this pretty girl was asking him to go swimming. Jessica ran back to Matt with a big smile. "Mom says it's okay for you to swim here with us."

Within twenty minutes, Matthew ran home for his swimsuit, got his dad's permission to take the afternoon off, and was in the pool with Jessica and her brothers. He had a wonderful afternoon swimming and talking to everyone. Jessica's father was in the area on business and her family was staying at the motel. That meant Jessica would be here all week! Matthew was really happy.

He and Evron talked at home that night. "I really like her Evron. I've never felt this way about anyone before, let alone a girl! I really like being with her!"

Evron smiled, "So this is a whole new experience for you, Matthew."

"It sure is. I can't wait to see her tomorrow."

Matthew and Jessica swam together at the pool all week. Sometimes she would walk over in the evening to the store for an ice cream cone, and they would sit outside and talk while watching his dad's customers come and go. They enjoyed watching all the different types of people and trying to guess what they might be like, what they did for a living, where they were coming from, or heading to. They laughed a lot and thoroughly enjoyed their times together.

On her last night at the motel, Matthew got enough nerve to ask Jessica if he could walk her home from the station.

"Sure, I'd like that, Matthew," she replied.

Matthew's heart was pounding as they neared the gates to the motel. "I'm going to miss you, Jessica," he stammered; "thanks for being so nice to me that first day and inviting me to swim."

"You're welcome, Matthew. I've really enjoyed having you as a new friend and I really like you too." She leaned forward and gave him a kiss on the cheek. Matthew thought he was going to faint; he was so happy.

"Let's exchange our addresses and telephone numbers so that we can stay in touch," gulped Matthew.

"That's a wonderful idea," replied Jessica, as she smiled back at him.

As he walked home that night, all he could think about was this new girl in his life. As soon as he got in the door, he told Evron about everything that happened. "Oh Evron, I'm going to miss her so much. It will be so boring without her! I have this beautiful feeling inside of me."

"Do you know what I think this is, Matthew?" Evron asked.

"What?" demanded Matthew.

"I think this is young love, Matthew. I think this is first love; it's sometimes called puppy love."

Matthew smiled shyly. "I think you're right. It sure beats my love for dirt bikes, snowboarding and basketball."

A Time for Evron

Matthew was cleaning up around the gas pumps when the two boys ran past and quickly flashed him some space comic magazines they had just shoplifted from his dad's store.

CHAPTER NINE

TESTING FRIENDSHIPS

BECAUSE OF THE EXCITEMENT over his father's new service centre, many of Matthew's school friends came to visit him and see everything that was going on. At first there was no problem, but, as time passed, some of his buddies took to hanging around and his dad had to have a talk with Matt.

"It's great that your friends are interested in you and the station, Matt," he said, "but they mustn't hang around too much. Not only does it keep you from your work, but it also doesn't appear business-like to customers."

"Okay, Dad," he replied. "I understand and I'll explain everything to them. They'll understand." And most of them did understand. There were two exceptions however: Jeremy and Sean. They were a bit older than the others and had a bad attitude at times. Only one week later, Matthew was cleaning up around the gas pumps when the two boys ran past and quickly flashed him some space comic magazines they had just shoplifted from his dad's store.

"Hey Matthew, your dad had freebies on today! What a great idea!" they laughed as they sped by. "Don't you dare squeal and get us in trouble."

Matthew was shocked and upset. He had heard rumors that

they had shoplifted from other stores, but he never thought they would do it from his own father. He worried all day about the incident and wasn't sure whether or not to tell his dad.

That night, he told Evron all the details and how he was torn between telling his father and not wanting to get his classmates into trouble. Evron thought about the dilemma for awhile and then said to Matthew, "These boys really must learn that, not only is shoplifting illegal, but also it hurts others. Your father loses his profit on those magazines he has already paid for. It is not fair to him and it's a dishonest act."

"I understand that," replied Matthew, "but they're my classmates, and I don't want to be accused of snitching on them."

"Well then," answered Evron, "you have a problem here. Which way do you turn?"

"I know what they did was wrong, but I'm scared to stand up to them."

Evron replied, somewhat briskly, "You must learn to live according to your own beliefs, Matthew, and face those who hurt others. You should tell your dad and see what he says. Your first responsibility is to him." Matthew reluctantly agreed to Evron's suggestion and waited for his dad to arrive home that night.

He spoke hesitantly, "Dad, I have to tell you about a problem I have."

"What's that, Matt?" his father asked with a worried look.

After Matthew told the upsetting story to his father, he waited in anticipation for what his dad would say. His father answered calmly, "I understand that you are torn between me and your classmates, Matthew. If they return the magazines, however, and apologize, I will not press shoplifting charges or involve the police. It's up to you whether or not to contact them again about this matter. I'll let you make the final decision. Let me know in the morning. Now try and get some sleep."

Matthew was thankful that his dad wasn't angry with him, but he still didn't know what to do. As he crawled into bed exhausted, Evron climbed up with him. Evron was silent for a while as he knew Matthew was very upset. Then he spoke. "Another way to look at this situation, Matthew, is that if your friends are forced to account for their misdeeds now, this could teach them a cheap lesson that might cost them a lot more later. In a way, you're doing them a favor by making them return the comics without a penalty."

"How's that?" asked Matthew.

"Well, suppose the next person to catch them stealing isn't as easy on them as your father will be. As they get older, they could be charged with theft and could get a criminal record. They could get off on the wrong foot. Many of their future jobs will require them to have absolutely no criminal charges on their records. It's good that they learn this lesson now."

Matthew got very little sleep that night. He thought over Evron's advice and knew that there was really only one right thing to do. He had to encourage the boys to return the comics and to apologize.

When Matthew confronted Jeremy and Sean the next day, they were at first unwilling to do anything. But after he presented Evron's arguments, they agreed to return the magazines. They respected Matt's determination to talk out the problem with them. Jeremy spoke quietly. "Thanks for caring about us this way Matt, especially after we did such a selfish thing to your dad."

"Yeah," continued Sean, "you're really a good friend, especially to two guys who can act like a couple of idiots at times."

Matthew's father was pleased at his son's decision to confront his classmates. He felt that it was better for Matthew to attack the problem head on rather than dodge around it. Matthew, too, was pleased that everything worked out. He was also thankful that his furry friend had been there to help him with his decision.

That night in bed, he gave Evron a big hug and kiss on his nose. "What would I ever do without you?" he asked. Evron smiled and hugged him back. That night they both slept soundly.

A Time for Evron

*Severe storm warnings had been issued earlier that morning,
but not serious enough to keep vehicles off the roads.
Slowly and gracefully, the beautiful tanker truck swung out
of the station, enroute to its day's deliveries.*

CHAPTER TEN

A NEW FRIEND

THE NEW SERVICE STATION turned out to be a very busy place that summer. People were constantly coming and going and, of course, the huge gasoline storage tanks for the pumps had to be filled regularly. This was done by enormous tanker trucks that continually traveled the country highways from one station stop to another.

One evening, a large red tanker truck rolled in. It was gleaming and even its huge chrome wheels were shining. Matthew loved looking at all the different kinds of trucks and cars, but this particular one really stood out. The truck driver was a very friendly man and he and Matthew were discussing his truck as he was hooking up all the huge hoses to fill the storage tanks. "How would you like to see the inside of the truck cab and its computer and radio systems?" he asked.

"Wow, would I ever!" replied Matt, as he eagerly climbed the big steps up to the cab. He had to hang on to the smooth chrome railing in order to keep his balance. When he got into the cab, it was glowing with all kinds of lights flashing on and off, and noisy from the squawking on the radio. It reminded him of the cockpit of an airplane.

Suddenly he heard movement beside him and noticed a boy just about his age waking up in a corner of the big front seat. "Hi," he said, "I guess I fell asleep. My name's Richard. Where's my dad?"

"If you mean the driver, he's in the office giving my dad the bills for the gasoline he just unloaded. By the way, my name's Matthew and my dad runs the gas station."

"Oh, cool!" replied Richard.

"We have a variety store here as well," said Matthew. "Would you like to have a Coke?"

"That would be great," replied Richard.

The boys entered the busy store and Matthew bought Richard a Coke. Then Richard's father came over to the boys and said it was time to leave. "Can Matthew come with us next week on our delivery run?" Richard asked his father.

"Sure, as long as his dad says it's okay."

Matthew's dad thought it was a great idea and it was agreed that he would be picked up at five in the morning the next Wednesday. Matthew was really excited and couldn't wait for the big day.

Five a.m. came early and it was barely getting light that Wednesday as the boys and Richard's father pulled away from the station. The boys wanted to bring Evron along as well and, because he was pretty small, everyone fit comfortably into the front cab of the truck.

Severe storm warnings had been issued earlier that morning, but they were not serious enough to keep vehicles off the roads. Slowly and gracefully, the beautiful tanker truck swung out of the station, enroute to its day's deliveries. Matt was in awe as Richard's dad easily guided the huge gearshift through its paces and soon had the rig up to top speed.

As time on the road passed, the boys and Richard's dad talked about the latest baseball standings, new sci-fi movies, and the upcoming school year. It was also fun to hear the other truck drivers talking on the CB radio. As usual, Evron was quiet in groups, but listened intently to all that was going on.

Just after lunch, about thirty kilometers from their next stop, they all noticed very dark storm clouds looming in the distance. Lightning began to appear in bright jagged streaks. When they turned down the cab radio, they could hear the sharp crack of nearby thunder. Everyone stopped talking and was quiet. Suddenly without warning, the huge truck drove into blinding rain and wind. Trees bowed and swayed and gushes of water appeared everywhere. The force of the rain was so heavy that they could barely see the road. The wipers weren't any help because the windshield was awash in constant spray.

Richard's dad began slowly to pull off the road to get to the safety of the curb. Suddenly, a yellow form loomed in front of them. There was a loud bump and the giant truck shook and groaned. Everyone was thrown forward. Evron had no seat belt and smashed against the dashboard. Richard's dad banged his head against the huge steering wheel. He was knocked unconscious and his nose was bleeding. The boys were dazed at first, but safely locked inside their seatbelts.

"Quick!" yelled Evron, "get out of the cab."

"Why?" replied Matthew. "We'll get soaked."

"I can smell gasoline," continued Evron. "If there's a spark, we could explode. I think our gas tanks have ruptured."

Richard thought he heard Evron speak, but was too upset to know for sure. He thought he was imagining things because of the shock of the accident. Now he was sobbing at the sight of his father slumped down on the seat.

"Quickly!" yelled Evron again; "unbuckle him and pull him outside his door."

The boys and Evron scrambled outside over to the driver's side of the cab. The door was jammed from the impact, but they slowly forced it back and dragged Richard's father out. He began to moan as the cold rain soaked him immediately.

"Further, further! Pull him further away from the truck!" commanded Evron.

Suddenly, a young child, no more than six years old, sat crying in front of them. As the boys stopped and looked around, they realized that the yellow form that had crashed into them was a school bus. Suddenly, they saw small children in tears everywhere.

Evron could see the lights of a nearby farmhouse at the end of a long driveway. "Matthew," he said, "listen to me carefully. We must get everyone to the safety of that house." Matthew couldn't see it through the millions of raindrops, but he trusted Evron's eyesight.

In all the confusion, Matthew finally found the schoolbus driver and together they gathered together the ten crying, wet children who had been coming home from a day camp. Richard's father was standing up now, and although still groggy, he could walk slowly. As the group climbed up onto the porch of the farmhouse, they heard loud explosions. Through the misty rain that had now almost stopped, they could see the schoolbus and tanker truck engulfed in flames and black smoke. The leaking gas had ignited with a spark from the school bus engine. Everyone was silent as they watched the huge ball of flames climb into the grey sky.

Stories of the horrible storm made headlines everywhere, but one of the most publicized events of the catastrophe was the tanker truck/schoolbus crash in which everyone had survived unharmed. Matthew and Richard were interviewed on television and portrayed as young heroes for leading everyone to safety. They both loved all the attention.

A few weeks later, Richard's dad had a new truck and was back on his gasoline run. Evron had a broken paw in a cast and was managing on three legs for the time being. Matthew and Richard became close friends as the lazy summer continued.

One afternoon, while they were sitting together in the eating area of the station, Matthew said, "You know Evron, it was really you who first noticed the gasoline smell and hurried us all to safety. You're the real hero."

"I know" replied Evron, grinning, "but I'm older than you are and I must admit, you're learning fast. I don't mind sharing the glory." He winked as Matthew ran off to help a new customer.

Matthew was very upset. Richard had said nothing during the fight, but Matthew knew he must be deeply hurt. When he did look at Richard, he saw that his eyes were downcast.

CHAPTER ELEVEN

MORE PROBLEMS

ONE OF THE BIG EVENTS SIGNALING the approaching end of summer holidays was the annual carnival which was set up in the town park. Everyone looked forward to it with great anticipation. There was everything for kids there, from the huge roller coaster and ferris wheel rides, to many games of chance and cotton candy floss.

By now, Richard and his family had moved to town because it was closer to his dad's delivery routes and they liked the small town atmosphere. Richard's parents had bought a small house two streets over from Matthew's house. They couldn't get over how quiet it was compared to the hustle and bustle of the big city where they had lived before.

Matthew was excited about taking his new friend to the carnival opening night. In addition to the normal excitement, there were fireworks as well that evening. Matthew also hoped to introduce Richard to some of his classmates who would certainly be there.

Richard and Matthew arrived just after the carnival gates opened. They bought their books of ride tickets immediately and quickly rushed up the main midway. It was rapidly filling up with excited kids and it was thrilling to hear the loud music and see the bright flickering lights on the rides.

Because the line ups for the rides were still short, the two boys were like the proverbial kids in a candy shop, quickly finishing one ride and then running to hop on another. In barely one hour, they had been on most of the rides once and were now starting to line up a second time for some of the bigger ones.

"Wow," said Richard, "is this ever fun! I wish we'd had this sort of thing where I lived before."

"Well, it only comes here once a year," replied Matthew; "so we better enjoy it while we can."

Just then, two of Matt's classmates approached them as they waited in line. "Hi guys," yelled Matthew. "How's it going?"

"We're doing great," answered Serge. "We just ate tons of free candy floss and now we're going to go on more rides."

"Who's this guy with you, Matthew?" asked Ben.

"Oh, this is a new friend I met this summer. His name is Richard," replied Matthew. "Richard, this is Serge, and this is Ben. They're going to be in our new class at school next week."

"It's nice to meet you guys," said Richard somewhat shyly.

Then Ben said, "Why don't you let us get into line with you two, Matthew? After all, a little butting in never hurt anyone," he laughed loudly.

"Well, uh, I don't think we'd better do that," replied Matthew. "We've all been waiting a long time and it's not really fair to these people behind us."

"Hey, c'mon," continued Serge; "what difference do two more make?"

"It makes a lot of difference to me," snapped the man in line behind the boys; "just get to the back of the line like everyone else."

"Geez, thanks a lot," replied Serge, as he glared at Matt. "Some friend you are. Just 'cause you have a new friend doesn't mean you can dump us now."

"There's nothing I can do," replied Matthew unhappily. "Let's not make a big deal about this."

"Oh sure," quickly answered Ben. "That's real easy for you to say. Especially now since you have a new friend. By the way, what's that funny thing on his head?"

"It's called a kieppah," replied Richard.

"Are you cold or something?" laughed Ben.

"It's a religious symbol," continued Richard. "I'm Jewish."

"Ooh ah" said Serge. "I don't think we have any Jews living around here. In fact, I don't think I've ever met a Jew before."

"Is your dad a lawyer or something?" asked Ben.

"No, why do you ask that?"

"Oh, I think my dad said all Jews were lawyers or doctors."

"Not at all," replied Richard. "Actually my father is a truck driver."

"Oh boy, a Jewish truck driver. What next?" kidded Ben.

Matthew heard all the cruel words, but couldn't believe his ears. "Just why are you guys going on like this?" he cried. Now he was really upset.

"Well maybe you think Jewish friends are special," answered Ben, "but we don't think so. In fact, maybe Jews aren't even so nice for that matter. After all, there are no other Jewish kids around here, so why do we need any now?"

Matthew was shocked, hearing what they were saying. He had never thought of Richard as different. Now his old friends were making a big deal out of nothing and picking on Richard for no reason.

"Stop talking like that!" he shouted at them. "Richard's being my new friend and also being Jewish has nothing to do with this! Now cut it out!"

"You're not our friend, anymore," yelled Serge. "You can get lost as far as we're concerned. We don't care about the ride anyway."

The two boys pushed off into the crowd.

Matthew was very upset. Richard had said nothing during the fight, but Matthew knew he must be deeply hurt. When he did look at Richard, he saw that his eyes were downcast.

"I'm sorry for the way they acted," stammered Matthew.

"Oh, don't worry about it," replied Richard. "It happens at times."

"What does?" asked Matt.

"Oh, you know, people making racist remarks."

"Well, I am worried about it," continued Matthew. "I've never experienced it before and I'm really upset that you had to get such a poor welcome from some of my school friends."

The fight was not discussed anymore that night, but both boys were still troubled.

After the park closed, and by the time Matthew had walked with Richard to his house and then got home himself, he was emotionally exhausted. He didn't know whether to tell his dad about the problem or not. However, he couldn't wait to tell Evron. He said good night to his dad and was soon in bed with Evron, recounting all the events of the evening and especially the trouble with his friends. Evron listened carefully as usual to all of Matt's feelings regarding this painful situation.

Evron said to Matthew, "What do you think you should do about this?" Matt thought for a moment, then replied, "I don't know; maybe I should get dad to talk to their parents, or would that be too much like squealing?"

"Well," said Evron, "if at all possible, do you think you could try to deal with it yourself?"

"Well, how can I do that?" asked Matthew. "I already spoke to them at the fair."

"I know, but that was with Richard there. Why not speak to them by themselves, with no one else around?"

"Oh Evron, I'm not so sure it will do any good."

A Time for Evron

"As a matter of fact," continued Evron, "it's probably best to start out by speaking to Ben alone. He's the one you said started it all."

"That's right," sighed Matthew; "but why just Ben alone?"

"Well, sometimes people are less honest and more like showoffs if others are watching them. If you speak to Ben alone, one to one, friend to friend, then I feel he's more likely to appreciate and consider more carefully his remarks about Richard. If he is really your friend, then he will listen seriously to someone who is upset with him."

"Okay." Matthew was watching Evron with a worried look. "I'll ride my bike to his house tomorrow."

The next day Matthew was nervous as he approached Ben's house and knocked on the door. Ben answered and both boys went out to the backyard for their talk. Ben's first reaction to Matthew's complaints about racial comments was "It's no big deal Matthew, really."

"Well," replied Matt, "it's a big deal to me."

They talked back and forth for about half an hour.

At one point, Ben said, "but my dad talks about Jews that way sometimes."

Evron had warned Matthew that Ben might use this type of excuse to justify his own bad behavior.

"That's no excuse," replied Matthew quickly, remembering what Evron had said. "You must learn to think for yourself and listen to those who are upset by your behavior. If I'm upset with you, then look seriously at why. As my friend, you have upset me and I'm telling you why!"

Ben thought about all of this very quietly. Matthew was an old and good friend whom he didn't want to lose. Maybe he had been a bit jealous that Matt had a new friend, but that was still no reason to make a nasty comment about Richard. After all, he wouldn't want someone doing the same to him. He realized that he had reacted impulsively in the heat of the moment.

"I'm glad you came to see me," Ben told Matthew. "I promise I won't treat Richard like that again. I want to speak to Serge as well. I started the trouble, but he followed along. Neither of us did a good thing. Are we still friends?"

"You bet," replied Matt.

Ben continued, "Do you think we should apologize to Richard ourselves, Matt, or could you just tell him for us?"

Matt thought carefully for a moment. "What do you think is best, Ben? What do you think Richard would appreciate most?"

"I'm sure he'd like to hear the apology from us directly, wouldn't he?"

"I think that's a good decision, Ben. I think it's better coming from you two face to face. I guess you could say it makes it more sincere."

"Okay, Matt, fair enough; I'll take care of it," Ben responded.

They shook hands and Matt rode off home. He was happy and relieved that everything had worked out better than he had expected. He also felt a new confidence in helping Ben come to a decision on his own. "Wow," he thought to himself, "I'm starting to sound a bit like Evron," as he smiled quietly. When he got home, Evron was waiting for him on the front porch.

"Hi Evron! Everything's okay with Ben. He says he's glad we talked. I'm glad I worked this out by myself as you suggested."

"I'm glad too. Hopefully, you both have learned a good lesson. Ben has learned to accept responsibility for his bad behavior and you've learned to speak up for yourself when you feel something is wrong."

Matthew felt pleased with himself as he and Evron rode off to his dad's service station. It was soon time for his afternoon shift to begin. He was thinking about Richard on the way. He hoped there wouldn't be any more trouble with his other class-mates this coming school year.

At that moment, Richard pointed to the water's surface
and asked, "Is that what happened to that one?"

CHAPTER TWELVE

FISHY BUSINESS

THE NEW SCHOOL YEAR was off to a good start and Matthew and his classmates were comfortably settling in with their new teacher, Mr. Sobalsky. For the first few weeks, Mr. Sobalsky had seemed very serious and rarely smiled, but, toward the end of the month, he seemed to be happier and even cracked the odd joke.

Matthew and many of his friends were scared of him at first. When Matt told Evron about his fears, Evron said that Mr. Sobalsky was probably only trying to instill some early discipline into the class so that the students weren't too relaxed. Evron even suggested that Mr. Sobalsky might be a bit afraid of the class himself and was, therefore, running a "tight ship" at first. The class was learning, with this new teacher, that there was a time for serious study and hard work, but there was also time for joking and fun.

September had been unseasonably warm and everyone was still really occupied with summer thoughts. One warm Sunday afternoon, Matt and Richard were sitting on the front porch talking and the topic of fishing came up. Much to Matt's surprise, he learned that Richard had never been fishing in his life. He certainly was a real city boy. They both quickly decided that, since it was such a beautiful day, they would go down to the nearby river and Matthew would teach Richard to fish.

Matt ran into the garage and found both his own and his dad's old fishing rods. Then they started digging in the garden for worms. There were two things Matthew hated about fishing - putting the worms on the hook and taking the fish off the hook. He loved the thrill of feeling the fish tug on his line and bringing them up to the water's surface, but he always wanted to take them carefully off the hook and gently throw them back, without hurting them.

After letting their parents know where they were going, both boys and Evron headed down to the nearby river. The river ran through the industrial side of town where there were manufacturing plants that produced such things as paint and paint supplies, car parts, and packaging materials such as plastic bags and food containers. Although the surrounding scenery wasn't as attractive as a quiet lake with hills and trees, it was still a popular fishing spot for the local kids and many adults.

Richard thought it was pretty 'icky' putting the worm on the hook, but he carefully followed Matthew's instructions and was assured that worms feel no pain. Both boys watched intently while their fishing bobbers twitched on the water's surface as the fish nibbled on the worms below.

Suddenly, Richard's bobber disappeared below the surface and he was intently tugging on his fishing pole in order to bring his wiggly fish out of the water. Matthew showed him how to remove the hook carefully from the fish's mouth before gently freeing it back into the water. Matthew explained how important it was not to damage the fish; otherwise it would be susceptible to infection and disease and would eventually die. At that moment, Richard pointed to the water's surface and asked, "Is that what happened to that one?" Both boys stared at a big fish that was floating belly up about six feet off shore. Then they counted three more dead fish floating nearby.

Matthew steered one of the dead fish to shore with his pole and then he and Richard carefully examined it. There seemed to be no outer indications of cuts or slashes. It looked perfectly normal although a bit bloated. Within an hour, the boys had pulled in a dozen more fish. All appeared normal on the outside, but all of them were very dead.

Matthew put six of these dead fish in his fish pail and took them home. In the evening, when his dad arrived home from the service centre, Matt told him all about his adventures that day. He was disappointed that his father didn't seem too upset about the dead fish, but he also realized that his dad had been working long hours and was very tired.

"Why not take them to school tomorrow and show Mr. Sobalsky?" said Evron. "As your teacher, he'll be interested in your concerns and may have some answers for you about possible causes for their deaths."

"Great idea," replied Matthew as he carefully sealed the fish pail and then busied himself preparing for his next school day.

Matthew and his dead fish soon became the big topic of the school on Monday morning. His teacher was not only very interested in Matthew and Richard's discovery, but he was also very concerned about what had possibly killed the fish.

Mr. Sobalsky had planned to start the class on Independent Study Units (I.S.U.'s) this week; so, he suggested to Matthew and Richard that this would be a good topic for them. Each group was to have three or four student members and would pick a topic to present to the class. Another classmate, named Sylvie, was interested in joining their group. Together the three of them began planning their investigation into the death of the fish.

Mr. Sobalsky suggested that they start by sending some water samples from the river to the Department of Health for testing. He also proposed that they make appointments to interview someone from each of the companies who had property on the river. One purpose of these interviews would be to find out how the plant processors disposed of waste materials. The students were pleased with their teacher's advice and impressed by how organized he was.

By the end of the week, Richard, Sylvie and Matthew had sent their water samples off in the mail and had made all the arrangements for their interviews with the companies the following week. The three of them made a good team because they were all hard workers and Sylvie did especially well talking with the adults at the companies on the telephone. Her mom owned a dress shop in town; so Sylvie had lots of practice dealing with adult customers, both on the telephone and in person.

For their first company interview that following Tuesday, the three students met with Mr. Tweed in his office after school. They had their questions well prepared, and Mr. Tweed was very co-operative and informative. One question which they saved for the end of the interview was "Does your company empty any of its waste products into the nearby river?" Mr. Tweed quickly informed them that not only was this against the law, but that the company also followed the strictest environmental guidelines and would never do any dumping. After half an hour, the young people thanked Mr. Tweed for his time and congratulated themselves on the way home about how well they had done. At first, they had all been a bit nervous about doing the interview, but Mr. Sobalsky had helped them with many of the questions. The previous night, when Matthew couldn't sleep from worrying about the impending interview, Evron had told him, "Not to worry, your two friends will be there with you. You have all prepared well, and it's good experience for you later when you will have to be interviewed for future part-time and summer jobs. It's really never too early to start gaining exposure to situations like this. It will boost your self-confidence." Now that the first interview was over, Matthew knew Evron was right. He was already feeling more at ease about the second interview and wasn't nearly as tense.

Two weeks later, when Matthew arrived home to find a letter

from the Department of Health waiting for him, he could hardly contain his excitement. It felt different to see such an important looking envelope addressed to himself. He opened the letter carefully and began to read. There were at first a lot of numbers listed, but the final sentences read:

> "In conclusion, we are alarmed at the inordinate levels of PCB's in the above categories. These would seem to be far above the range which would normally be found in bodies of water of this nature and in this area. It is our conclusion that these levels could cause the high death rate of fish in the same area. Someone from the Ministry will be contacting you in the near future."

Matthew had to look up the word "inordinate" in his dictionary. It meant " not normal". "Wow," he thought, "so maybe we're onto something after all." He couldn't wait to tell Mr. Sobalsky and the class about the letter. Evron was excited about it too.

The next day, Matthew arrived early at school and immediately showed his teacher the letter. He was initially surprised at Mr. Sobalsky's reaction. He was very quiet and seemed deep in thought. Then he said, "I think we have a problem here, Matthew."

"For sure," replied Matt, "but we suspected something like this was killing the fish."

"Yes, but according to all your group interviews so far, no company is dumping any wastes into the river, right?"

"That's right," replied Matthew.

"Then I ask you, Matthew, my young researcher, where are all the pollutants coming from? Is someone lying to you, or are these pollutants from another source you haven't checked out yet?"

"Oh, I get it," said Matthew. "Now this is getting more complicated."

"Yes," replied Mr. Sobalsky. "This is becoming a very complicated and very interesting I.S.U."

The following days were a blur of events for Matthew, Richard, Sylvie and their class. When the Ministry people found out that Matthew was only a young student and not an adult, they told him that some adult representing him would have to be their contact person. His teacher and trusted advisor was Matthew's logical choice. Thus Mr. Sobalsky became the key figure in the ensuing "pollution investigation."

When news of the problem and investigation leaked out, the reaction in their town was widespread and varied. Some people thought it was "no big deal"; others wanted the people responsible for the pollution charged with a criminal offense. The local newspapers were full of this issue every week and Matthew, Richard, Sylvie, his class, and their teacher all became well known by means of the T.V. and radio. There were even interviews on the local T.V. channel with Mr. Sobalsky and the kids, as well as pictures of the school.

One evening, after Matthew's dad arrived home quite late, he had a quick bite to eat and then went into Matthew's bedroom as he was getting ready for bed. "Matt, I need to speak to you for a minute," his dad said very seriously.

"Sure," replied Matthew. He could tell his father was upset. He and Evron listened intently to his dad's words.

"I'm having some difficulties at the service station with some of my customers. A few are making remarks that it's too bad my son is causing so much trouble with his big pollution investigation. They wonder if you realize that, if some of these companies are charged with dumping, they may have to close down and people could lose their jobs. They're also saying that people who lose jobs won't need to buy gasoline from me anymore, and maybe their friends won't either."

Matt was totally stunned by his father's words. He had never,

ever thought that this investigation could ever trouble his father. "Oh my gosh," he gasped, "who would ever think adults would threaten you? I'm shocked."

"Well Matthew," his father replied, "adults can be very cruel and immature at times, just like kids. I guess I'm asking you to go easy on this pollution investigation. I know you're caught up in it, but think about taking a lower profile or perhaps letting Mr. Sobalsky take all interviews. Maybe you kids should leave it to the adults now and stay out of it."

"Okay Dad, I'll see what the others say; I'm sorry about the trouble."

Matt's dad hugged him goodnight and then left.

Matthew was very quiet and sad. He was upset that this had happened to his father, but he was also upset that he might have to leave the investigation. He confided in Evron. "I have put a lot of time and effort into this. So have Richard and Sylvie. I'm enjoying our responsibilities in the project and I'm enjoying what we've accomplished. I'm proud that Richard and I originally started it all. Why should I give it all up now? Do you think I'm being selfish? Is this being inconsiderate of my father's feelings?"

Evron tried to make a joke. "Well, you sure are caught between a rock and a hard place."

Matthew didn't laugh.

"Seriously though," Evron continued, "you are totally correct. You and Richard have initiated a worthwhile and productive investigation. If you've made certain people uncomfortable, then so be it. You haven't caused the pollution; you are investigating the problem. Your group, Mr. Sobalsky, and the Ministry are trying to solve the problem. If some people and companies have to take a hard look at themselves, then it is for the betterment of the environment and for all of us in the long run."

"Well I'm glad you agree with me. But what about my dad?"

Bryan Smillie

Evron answered quietly, "I think the best way to handle this is to let him know again how badly you feel for him and that you understand his concern. Tell him that you'll tell the others about some of his problems, but don't mention he wanted you all out of the investigation. Hopefully, from now on, you and the group won't get as much exposure anyway. This issue has a life of its own now without you. The proper authorities are involved and it has nothing to do with you anymore."

"You don't think we should get out ?" asked Matt.

"No way. You've done the right thing. Your father is naturally very upset about his own difficulties, but you shouldn't have to give up doing what you feel is right. I think this situation will resolve itself without the students having to be involved much more."

As it turned out, Evron was right. By the end of the month, the Ministry had concluded its investigation and the source of the poisonous chemicals was found. Workers in one of the plants had been dumping excess liquid waste into the river when their own special waste removal tanks were full. Rather than telling management of the overflow problem, and stopping production while waiting for fresh empty tanks to be delivered, they had just directed the waste hoses toward the river. Illegal dumping charges and fines had been laid against the company and the workers, but no jobs were lost.

Matthew, Richard and Sylvie were soon heralded as town heroes. Their pictures again were everywhere and the mayor presented them with special "Environment Awareness Awards".

When presenting the awards, the mayor said, "We are proud of all our young people today. It is reassuring that even the very young are interested in keeping our planet clean for future generations, and are sometimes able to help adults solve these difficult problems."

Mr. Sobalsky was naturally proud of his special group of students. He called them his "junior scientists." Although there had been some excellent I.S.U. presentations that term, Matt, Richard and Sylvie achieved the top marks in the class. He asked only one favor of them. "Perhaps your next I.S.U. project will not take up quite so much class time." Everyone laughed and congratulated the happy trio.

That night, as Matthew and Evron lay in bed talking, Evron said, "I'm proud of you, Matthew. You took an initial concern and researched the problem. You enlisted the help of others, stuck by your convictions with your father, and carried through your commitment to a successful conclusion. This is a big accomplishment for a young person."

"Thanks, Evron," Matthew replied proudly, and gave him a big hug.

*Matt and Richard were really shocked when Sylvie's mom
turned the "OPEN" sign around to "CLOSED".
Obviously she did not want anyone disturbing them.*

CHAPTER THIRTEEN

BAD GIRLS

SYLVIE HAD BECOME GOOD FRIENDS with Matthew and Richard over the course of the I.S.U. project. At their age, girls and guys didn't often hang out together much, but because of having to work together, they often would spend time at each other's homes, plotting their interviews and working on organizing the project. Times like these were fun too because it gave the kids time to meet each other's parents. Like Matthew, Sylvie was from a single parent family and he thought her mom was "cool", bubbly, and very young for a mom.

One afternoon, as Matt and Richard walked through town on their way home from school, Sylvie's mom came out of her store to say hello to them. "Hi boys, how are things going?"

"Fine," replied Matt.

"Much quieter," continued Richard, "now that our I.S.U. project is finished." They all laughed.

Then Sylvie's mother became very serious and said, "I wonder if you boys would mind coming into the store for a few minutes. I have a few things I would like to discuss with you."

"Sure thing," replied Matt and they all entered through the front doorway of the attractive shop. Matt and Richard were really shocked when Sylvie's mom turned the "OPEN" sign around to "CLOSED". Obviously she did not want anyone disturbing them.

"I want to ask you boys a few questions about school and I want you please to be honest with me."

The boys looked at each other in surprise.

"I've noticed for the past couple of months since school started that Sylvie seems very tense and agitated at times. She'll often snap at me or burst into tears without any reason. This is very out of character for her. Also, she normally gets ten dollars a week allowance for things like milk and snacks at school, but lately she's been asking for fifteen dollars a week because she says she needs more money for other things. It didn't make much sense to me," she continued, "but when I questioned her about this, she got really upset and started to cry. This is just not like Sylvie."

"Wow," replied Richard, "that doesn't seem like her to me either." Matt agreed.

"So, last week when I was clearing her school bag and notebooks off the dining room table, a note fell out on the floor. Here it is; please read it." Both boys read the note and stared at each other in disbelief:

> "Sylvie,
> You are late with the money this week. Bring it to us tomorrow or you are in big trouble.
>
> THE BAD GIRLS"

They had heard of older kids in small gangs threatening the younger ones for lunch money, but had never actually seen it being done. This note sure changed things. "Wow," stammered Matt, "we've heard of this happening, but only through rumors."

"Yeah," continued Richard, "now it seems it's getting really close to us."

They explained to Mrs. Becker about the rumors of gangs in the school at the higher grade levels and how they would threaten younger students for "safe money". "Safe money" was supposed to guarantee that the younger kids wouldn't be beaten up or that their more valuable coats, book bags or pocket computers wouldn't be "stolen" from them. Kids were also instructed to tell no one about the arrangement or they would be roughed up.

When the boys had finished explaining, Mrs. Becker was quietly crying. "Do you really think this is happening to Sylvie?" she asked.

"We're pretty sure," replied Matthew. Richard nodded in agreement. "What should I do?"

Matthew thought quietly for a moment and then replied. "Let Richard and I talk it over tonight and we'll get back to you tomorrow after school. We'll come up with some kind of plan; don't worry."

"Oh, thank you so much. I'm so glad someone else knows now. I was sick with worry."

Matthew wasn't exactly sure what they could do to help Sylvie, but he knew one thing: Evron would know what to do. That night after dinner, Evron, Matthew and Richard gathered in Matthew's bedroom. Richard hadn't seen Evron talk that much and it still amazed him when Evron spoke. After they told the whole story to Evron, he thought for a short while and then said. "I think the first thing you two should do is take Sylvie aside by yourselves and tell her about her mother's concerns and your suspicions about the extortion."

"What's 'extortion'?" asked Richard.

"That means taking money or property from someone dishonestly," replied Evron.

"I think you should be with us, Evron, when we talk to Sylvie," continued Matt.

"Yeah," added Richard, "you'll know better what to say to her than the two of us."

"Okay," replied Evron. "Let's speak to her here tomorrow after school."

"That's great," replied Matthew. "We'll tell her we have some follow up information to do on the I.S.U. project."

The next day after school, the three kids met in Matthew's kitchen. He got snacks for everyone and then brought Evron into the room. Sylvie, of course, knew Evron, but never as a talking dog. First, she was shocked by Evron's speaking and then, by the boy's knowledge of the money threats against her.

At first, she started to cry and said she didn't want to talk about it. Then, when she calmed down, Evron said, "We're here to help you Sylvie; you mustn't feel as if you have to tackle this problem alone. Anything we choose to do will only be with your permission. No one else will know anything about it."

Sylvie felt better and was happy that she could finally talk to others about her difficulties. The four of them talked about the situation for a couple of hours. Matt's father had left a large casserole in the oven for them; so the three kids shared dinner while they continued talking. As it turned out, a gang of three girls had been harassing Sylvie. She had been too frightened to speak to anyone about it.

Finally Evron said, "I think you three should talk to the girls alone at first, without involving parents and the school principal."

"But, Evron," Sylvie gasped, "that will probably only make them madder at me!"

"I don't think so. You must make them understand that you don't want to get them into further trouble, but only to stop them bothering you. Besides, they will also be aware now that Matt and Richard know as well. Who are these 'bad girls' anyway?"

"Oh, they're not very popular in the next grade, Evron," replied Sylvie. "Their parents don't seem to have much control over them. They can go out whenever they want, they have no curfews, and generally they have a bad reputation."

"Do any of your friends really know them?" asked Evron.

"Not really," replied Sylvie.

"We just know them by reputation," added Matthew.

A Time for Evron

"No one is really friendly with them," said Richard, "because they're not friendly with us."

"Okay, my suggestion," replied Evron, "is to invite them over here after school tomorrow, and the three of you sit down and talk with the three of them."

"You can't be serious," gasped Matthew. "Do you really believe they'll listen to us?"

"I think it's worth a try," replied Evron. "After all, what have you got to lose? If they get mad and walk out, then we're back to square one which is where we are right now anyway."

"Oh gosh, I don't know," groaned Richard.

"And besides," continued Evron, "once you get to know them better, you might be surprised at how nice they really are. Sometimes people live up to their bad reputations and what others think of them. Look at the way they signed the note to Sylvie: "THE BAD GIRLS". It's as if they accept it. If other students think they are tough and mean, maybe they just play this role. Let's see what happens if you're nice to them first, in spite of what they've done to Sylvie."

And so it was agreed that they would try to arrange a meeting with the three "bad girls" the next day. To everyone's shock and dismay, the "bad girls" agreed to come.

Matthew told his father about having the group over so, once again, his dad brought extra food and drinks home. Matthew was beginning to feel as if he were running a small restaurant.

It was agreed ahead of time that Sylvie and Richard and Matthew would do all the talking, and that Evron would stay out of it - just be a quiet, cute little doggy curled up on the floor. There was no need for everyone to know about him. Besides, he wanted his young friends to try to cope with this problem on their own.

At first the "bad girls" were mad that the boys knew about their scam, but they soon calmed down when they found out that no one wanted to carry it any further with their parents or the school. As they continued talking, the kids soon realized that they had many things in common. Sylvie and the girls all liked the same rock musicians, went "gah gah" over the same young movie stars, and basically liked the same pop music.

The "bad girls" really seemed to like talking to the others.

At this point, Evron crawled up on Matt's lap and appeared to be kissing him on his ear. The girls thought this was really cute. Evron was really whispering to Matthew. "The situation is as I had hoped," he said. "These girls probably only really wanted some positive attention paid to them, and some new people to talk to. Now I have another idea," he continued. "You know that 'lip sync' competition for charity you and the student council are running?"

"Yeah," whispered Matt.

"Why not encourage these girls to enter as part of the competition. Let them imitate some popular group. If Sylvie joins them, it will help them to break the ice and to be better accepted by the other students. Not only that, they'll now be involved in a fund-raising activity, raising money for hospitalized children, rather than stealing money from others."

"Okay," replied Matt. " That sounds great. You get down now and I'll pretend this was all my idea," he chuckled, as Evron jumped down to the floor.

The "bad girls" loved Matt's idea and Sylvie was only too happy to join the new group. Over the next few weeks, Sylvie and the girls spent many hours together practicing after school and in each other's homes. They got to meet each other's parents and the "bad girls" lives were not nearly as different as others might have thought.

Finally, competition day arrived and the whole school packed the auditorium for the big event. There was much screaming, laughing and cheering as ten groups gave their performances. Matt and Richard cheered loudest for the girls. When everyone had finished and the judging was completed, Sylvie's group took the second place prize. They were disappointed that they didn't place first, but everyone had had a wonderful time and the student body had raised over three hundred dollars for charity.

As the four girls walked home from school that day, Courtney said, "Sylvie, Alyssa, Shannon and I really want to thank you for being our new friend and for being in the competition with us. If you hadn't been so keen about going in it, I doubt if we would have done it. Not only that, but we feel a lot more comfortable now that we're accepted by the other students at school."

"Oh, that's okay," replied Sylvie. "I've really enjoyed it too and I'm glad I've made new friends with you."

"We also want to give you back your twenty-five dollars which we scammed from you over those past weeks. We're really ashamed we did this. We're learning it's a lot more fun giving and sharing with others. We're all much happier this way."

They all hugged each other good-bye at the corner. Sylvie was just about to head home when Courtney said, "Sylvie, before you go, there's one other thing we want to tell you." All three girls had their eyes downcast. Sylvie sensed there was still something wrong, perhaps some unfinished business. Courtney continued, "Do you know that small Asian girl who's new to the school this year? She often sits in the upstairs hallway at lunch hour. We don't think she has many friends and she doesn't speak English very well."

"Oh, I've seen her around a bit," replied Sylvie, "but not very much; she's in a younger grade than me."

Alyssa broke in, "She's very shy and keeps to herself a lot. She always seems to be studying or something. Her name is Wai-Jing."

There was a long silence, then Shannon continued. "Sylvie, we've been taking money from her too; oh, we've been so mean to her. We've been such bullies; I'm so ashamed." Tears were welling up in her eyes.

Sylvie looked at the three girls. They sure didn't look like the mean and nasty people she had known just a couple of weeks before.

"What can we do about this?" Sylvie asked sadly.

"Well, we were hoping you could come with us and talk to Wai-Jing," replied Shannon, as she wiped her eyes. "She's very scared of us. Maybe you could explain to her how sorry we are about how we've treated her. We've got her money to return to her too."

Sylvie thought quietly for a moment, then continued. "I could tell her how you guys treated me the same way and that now we're friends and you're sorry about everything."

"That would be wonderful, Sylvie," replied Courtney. "We hate to involve you, but we think it would make it easier for Wai-Jing to understand if you do the talking."

"Thanks so much," added Alyssa as she hugged Sylvie. "You're a great new friend."

The next day at lunch hour, the four girls approached Wai-Jing as she sat quietly in the upstairs hallway, reading a book. She was alone. She stared with a frightened look in her eyes at the approaching girls. Sylvie's heart ached; she knew the feeling all too well.

"Hi Wai-Jing, my name is Sylvie," she said softly as she crouched down beside her. Slowly she told Wai-Jing her own story and how sorry the three girls were about how they had treated them both. Wai-Jing began to relax and even forced a smile as she thanked Sylvie for returning her money.

Then Alyssa spoke. "If you would like, Wai-Jing, we want to treat you to lunch in the cafeteria today, if that's okay."

"Yes, thank you, very nice new friends," Wai-Jing replied in a soft voice. "It's nice to meet new girls." She had a beautiful smile.

After that day, Wai-Jing's four new friends made sure she was never alone at lunch hour. They often ate in the cafeteria together or walked over to the pizza parlor in town. As she spent more time with the girls, Wai-Jing's English began gradually to improve. She became more at ease and outgoing, and she was happy now to be at school each day.

One day after class, as Sylvie waved goodbye to her young friend boarding the school bus, she sighed deeply and said to herself, "Wow, it sure is nice to see her so much happier now. It's nice to know that just as people have helped me, I've been able to help someone else too."

*Mr. Burrows was halfway down the ladder when his foot
slipped off a rung and he started to tumble.*

CHAPTER FOURTEEN

A WAR HERO

MATTHEW LOVED THE LONG HOT SUMMER and always hoped those warm beautiful days would never end. Nevertheless, autumn arrived, and the days started getting shorter, the sun was much lower in the sky, and the air was much cooler. People on his street started putting away summer lawn furniture and, of course, raking leaves. The one thing Matt did like about fall was the smell of burning leaves. Everybody on his street raked their leaves to the curbside of their front yards and set them ablaze. Quite often, Matthew and some of the other boys made extra money by helping their neighbors rake the leaves. Old Mr. Burrows, who lived three houses down from Matt, sometimes paid him by the hour to do some raking. Although it was said that he was almost eighty years old, he was still very independent and healthy. His wife had died many years previously, and his children were all married and living in other cities.

Although Matt liked Mr. Burrows, he found him very grumpy at times. Sometimes, when Matthew was scheduled to do some work for him after school, Mr. Burrows would start the job before Matthew arrived home, and then complain that he couldn't wait any longer for Matt to arrive.

On this particular day, Matt and Mr. Burrows were planning to clear the fallen leaves from the eavestroughs. This was not a difficult job, but it could be a bit dangerous. Mr. Burrows would steady and hold the tall ladder while Matthew would scramble to the top, pull the leaves out of the eavestroughs and then climb back down. They would then move the ladder further along and repeat this procedure around the whole outside of the house.

But sure enough, on this day, just as Matthew rounded the corner from school, he spotted Mr. Burrows already up the ladder.

"Good afternoon, Matthew," Mr. Burrows said, as he looked down at Matthew from his high perch.

"Good afternoon, Mr. Burrows," replied Matthew, "how are you today?"

"I'm fine, thank you, but I wanted to get this job started early because it might rain tonight and I want the eavestroughs clear. We'll move the ladder now so that you can do the next section of cleaning."

Mr. Burrows was halfway down the ladder when his foot slipped off a rung and he started to tumble. Matthew saw him falling and made a desperate attempt to grab him. Mr. Burrows crashed into Matthew's shoulder and chest, as they both collapsed onto the ground. Matt gasped for breath, as Mr. Burrows was now lying on top of him and groaning. Matthew gasped, "Are you alright?"

"I, ... I don't know," moaned Mr. Burrows. "My arm is very sore. I think, ... I think I may have broken it."

"Don't move," yelled Matthew, as he wriggled from underneath Mr. Burrows's heavy body and scrambled to his feet. His own shoulder ached badly.

"Where are you going?" yelled Mr. Burrows, as Matthew headed for the front door.

A Time for Evron

"I'm going to call 911 and have them send an ambulance for you."

Mr. Burrows didn't reply. He seemed to be in shock as he just lay motionless on the ground.

The ambulance arrived within ten minutes and the old man was carefully bundled onto a stretcher. "Don't worry, Mr. Burrows," Matthew assured him. "I'll lock up the house for you and take care of your cat."

"Thanks Matthew," he whispered, as the stretcher was loaded into the ambulance. He seemed in too much pain even to speak.

As a result of Mr. Burrows's fall, he had a broken right arm, cracked ribs and lots of bruises. He was sent home from the hospital within two days, but his big disappointment was that he wouldn't be allowed to drive his car for at least one month. A nurse would come to visit every day to check on his medical condition.

On Mr. Burrows's first day home, Matthew dropped in on the way home from school to see how he was doing. He entered the living room where Mr. Burrows was watching television.

"Don't you ever knock before you enter?" snapped the old man.

"I did, Mr. Burrows, several times. I figured you couldn't hear me because of the T.V."

"There's nothing wrong with my hearing. Just my arm and ribs," the old man replied gruffly.

"I didn't mean that," sighed Matthew, "only that ..."

"Never mind," interrupted the old man. "Why are you here?"

"I just wanted to see how you are!"

"Well, I'm not that good as you can see," moaned Mr. Burrows. "And my chest aches all the time."

"Is there anything I can do for you? Can I buy you some groceries?"

"No, I don't need any groceries; I'm not even that hungry."

"I'll try and finish clearing the leaves up on my own, sir, or maybe bring a friend along to help me."

"No way you're going to bring any other friends around here, young man. I'm not paying two hourly wages; one is enough. If you can't do it on your own, don't bother!"

Matthew was quiet for a moment. Mr. Burrows had always been a bit grumpy, but now he was really bad. "Okay then," replied Matt, "I'll do it by myself. I'll be back later."

The old man said nothing as Matthew left quietly and headed for home.

As soon as he got home, he told Evron how mean and grouchy Mr. Burrows had been. "If he's going to be like that, he can get someone else to help him out and worry about him!" Matthew snapped.

Evron knew Matt had every reason to be angry. "I know how you feel, Matt, but think about him for a moment. He's just got home from the hospital, he's sore all over, and he can't drive his car for at least one month. Not only that, he realizes he should have waited for you and that it's his own fault he has hurt himself."

"Yeah, ... well obviously, I can't cheer him up," replied Matt.

"Well, not just yet," continued Evron, "but I'll bet he'll be different in a couple of days ... you'll see!"

"No I won't!" snapped Matthew, "because I'm not going back to see him."

"Well, if that's your decision, that is a very immature way to treat him."

"Why?" asked Matthew.

"Because you are becoming as miserable and obstinate as he is!"

"So, what do you suggest I should do, old wise one?" replied Matthew, as he started to smile.

"Well, I think the first thing you should do is to buy him

some fresh milk and fruit tomorrow on the way home from school. Don't even ask him to pay for it. Just say it's your treat."

"Are you sure?" gulped Matthew. "What if he gets mad?"

"He won't; he'll be very glad to see you."

"What am I going to do about clearing the leaves then? I can't go up the ladder alone."

"I suggest you ask Richard to help you and tell Mr. Burrows that Richard is helping you out free of charge."

"I can't ask Richard to help me for nothing."

"No, you shouldn't do that, but tell him you will split your hourly wage with him."

"I'm not sure he'll go for it," replied Matthew.

"Oh, I think he will," answered Evron. "He'll do it as a favor for you as his friend. Besides, you tell me he likes Mr. Burrows anyway."

"Yeah, but he's never tried working for him," retorted Matthew.

The next day, Matthew arrived at Mr. Burrows's house, gave him the groceries, and waited for the response.

"Thank you very much, Matthew; that was very thoughtful of you!" said Mr. Burrows. "I'm sorry I was irritable with you yesterday. I slept much better last night and I'm feeling a lot stronger today."

"You're very welcome, Sir."

The old man continued, "If you have time tomorrow, there are a few other items I would like you to pick up and I'll give you the money for everything."

"Okay," replied Matt, "that's great."

Matthew was just about to ask him about Richard helping him out with the leaves when Mr. Burrows said, "And about your friend helping you out, I think that's a great idea and I'll be more than willing to pay him just as I pay you."

"Wow!! That's great, Mr. Burrows!"

"Actually, Matthew, I'm very fortunate to have two trustworthy boys like you and your friend to help me out."

When Matt got home, Evron was waiting, of course, to find out what had happened. "Oh Evron," Matt exclaimed, "he was so nice today - what a difference! I guess he was so miserable yesterday because of the shock of the accident."

"Not only that," replied Evron, "but I'll bet he realizes how much he'll need your help for awhile."

"I shouldn't have been as mad at him as I was; I guess I reacted too quickly."

Evron smiled at him.

Mr. Burrows, Matt and Richard became closer over the next few weeks. Once the boys finished the leaves, he had them clean out the flower beds, put some storm windows on the house, and put out the garbage and recycling containers each week.

One day after working at Mr. Burrows's house, they were about to leave when he asked, "How would you boys like to stay for a barbeque tomorrow after you've finished your chores? It won't be anything fancy, just hot dogs and hamburgers."

Richard and Matthew looked at each other. "That sounds great Mr. Burrows!" answered Matthew.

"I don't see a problem, Sir," added Richard. "We'll just have to ask our parents first."

"That's swell, fellas; then if I don't hear back from you tonight, I'll assume you are coming tomorrow after school."

On the way home, Matt and Richard talked about this latest development. They were sort of surprised at his kindness and yet the old man did seem to enjoy their company.

When Evron heard the latest news, he said, "I think you boys have become Mr. Burrows's new young friends. Everyone needs to be connected to someone, to share his life with someone. You two help fulfill this need for him at this time."

A Time for Evron

The big day for the old gentleman's presentation arrived and he came to class well prepared.

CHAPTER FIFTEEN

A GUEST TEACHER

OVER THE NEXT FEW WEEKS, Matt and Richard visited Mr. Burrows frequently. Sometimes they had dinner together, or sometimes the boys just stopped for a short chat on the way home from school.

One evening, while the boys were visiting after dinner, Mr. Burrows started talking about some of his family pictures in his living room. The boys were fascinated by a big picture of an armored tank that hung over his fireplace. They were astonished when Mr. Burrows said, "I was a gunner in that tank in the Second World War. That's a Sherman tank and they were used a lot by the Allies in the war to fight the enemy!"

"Wow," gasped Richard, "you were in World War II?"

"I sure was," proudly replied the old man.

"What are Allies?" asked Matt.

"They were the armies that fought together against the Germans."

"Oh," interjected Richard. "I think Mr. Sobalsky mentioned that word in class yesterday. We're starting to study the Second World War in history class now."

"That would be correct," answered Mr. Burrows. "The allies were composed of groups of soldiers such as the British, French,

Americans, Canadians and many others."

"Were you actually in Germany?" asked Richard.

"No," replied the old gentleman, "my regiment spent most of the time fighting in Italy. Don't forget the Germans had started taking over many countries in Europe and, towards the end of the war, Italy was one of them."

"So were you trying to get the Germans out of Italy?" asked Matt.

"That's right," replied Mr. Burrows. "We fought the enemy on various parts of Italian soil."

"Italian soil?" questioned Richard.

"Yes, that's a term often used for land when referring to the various battles of a war."

"Oh," replied the boys together. They were starting to learn some really interesting stuff from Mr. Burrows.

"Did you ever shoot anyone and kill him?" asked Richard.

"I probably did," the old gentleman replied, "but, because I was shooting from the tank, I was a long distance away from my target; so, I never actually saw someone get killed."

"What kind of target would you hit?" asked Matt.

"Well, sometimes I shot at enemy tanks, or fired shots into a building where the enemy was hiding. Then it would be almost certain that the soldiers in those spots were killed."

The boys were spellbound all evening as Mr. Burrows continued with his wartime stories. The old gentleman in front of them was now being transformed, in their minds, into a young fighting soldier with his tales of life in action in World War II.

When Matthew finally got home that night, he was still excited as he told Evron all about the latest news regarding Mr. Burrows. Evron listened intently to Matt's story then exclaimed, "I have a great idea!"

"Oh, oh," replied Matt. "Whenever you have a great idea, it

usually means I'm going to get involved in some new plan you have. So what is it now?"

Evron smiled back at Matt. "Why don't you take Mr. Burrows to school?"

"What? An old gentleman in our class? Why, he's old enough to be our grandfather."

"I realize that," replied Evron, "but think of all the knowledge he has; think of all he has seen in life!"

"Yes, but we already have a teacher to tell us all this history," answered Matt.

"This isn't the same; your teacher is young. He hasn't lived through the Second World War. He hasn't experienced actual battles, firing weapons, killing people, seeing death and destruction. He hasn't lived cramped up in a hot battle tank all day."

Matthew was listening intently as Evron continued. "Look at how excited you were when you came home tonight. Why not let Mr. Burrows excite the whole class with his stories?"

"Maybe you're right," Matt replied. "After all, we are taking World War II in history now."

The next day, Matthew relayed Evron's suggestions to Mr. Sobalsky, who was delighted with the idea and felt the whole class would benefit from the visit. Matthew asked his teacher to write a note inviting Mr. Burrows to speak to the class and Matthew would deliver it. He knew the old gentleman well enough to know that he alone would never be able to talk Mr. Burrows into attending the class.

That afternoon after school, Matt gave Mr. Burrows the letter. He watched intently as the old gentleman slowly read the note. "That's very nice of you and your teacher to invite me," replied Mr. Burrows, "but your classmates won't want to listen to an old man."

"That's not true, Mr. Burrows. Richard and I like listening to your stories and so will others."

"Well, let me think it over and I'll let you know."

"That's great; thanks a lot, Sir," replied Matthew.

It took Mr. Burrows a couple of days before he got back to Matthew with his answer. He did agree to speak to the class.

The big day for the old gentleman's presentation arrived and he came to class well prepared in his old uniform. He brought his old war pictures, his regiment medals, his actual old water canteen, his helmet and some of his food dishes the soldiers carried in their backpacks. He was a great collector of books on the war; he had even more than the school library and he brought these along as well. Some of the pictures were of Mr. Burrows as a young man in the war. Many of the kids found it hard to believe that this old fellow was the same one as in the pictures.

"Boy," said Sean, "this makes history much more interesting now that I know someone who was actually in the war."

"Yeah," added Kathryn, "my dad was born after the war and my grandpa is dead. I've never known anyone who was in the war."

Mr. Burrows's presentation was supposed to last only one hour until recess. However, the students were so excited that they missed recess and Mr. Sobalsky agreed to let them spend the whole afternoon with Mr. Burrows. Many students were sad to see him leave at the end of the day.

"Can you come back next week?" asked Caitlin.

"Well maybe not that soon," responded Mr. Burrows, "but perhaps again next term."

"That would be wonderful," added Mr. Sobalsky. "Thank you so much for coming, Sir. You have really given the students something to talk about tonight over the dinner table."

Mr. Sobalsky asked Matt if he would stay for a few minutes after school so that he could speak to him. "Thanks so much for thinking of asking Mr. Burrows to class Matthew. The students really enjoyed him. He's such a nice fellow. And he gets along so well with young people."

"You're welcome, Sir," answered Matt, as he headed for the door.

On his way home, Matt thought to himself, "Yeah, he sure was friendly and happy today; too bad he's not like that all the time. And thanks for thanking me, Mr. Sobalsky, but you really should thank Evron."

Matt decided to drop by Mr. Burrows's house on the way home. He wanted to talk to him, but without the other students around.

"I really enjoyed your presentation today, Mr. Burrows."

"Thanks Matt. I realize how much happier I am when I'm interacting with people. I tend to get too grumpy when I'm by myself. It's nice to talk to others and to know they are interested in me. It makes me feel more valuable than just sitting around by my lonesome, feeling sorry for myself. I guess we all like to feel needed by others."

"Well, we all really enjoyed you, Sir. Bye for now."

After dinner that night, Evron and Matt were playing ball in the backyard. They paused for a break and were sitting quietly watching the early evening sun go down.

"I've just been thinking about Mr. Burrows and how much fun we all had today," said Matt.

"Yes. It sure worked out well," replied Evron.

"I have a great idea," continued Matthew, "and guess what? You didn't have to give it to me!"

"Then what makes you think it's so great?" Evron kidded.

"Well, you just tell me," joked Matt.

"Okay, go ahead; I can hardly wait to hear."

Matt continued. "What if ... are you ready?" Evron nodded. "What if other kids in the class brought in other older guests who could tell us about their life stories?"

"Like who?" asked Evron, encouraging Matthew.

"Well, suppose it was someone else from the war - maybe someone who was a prisoner of war. What about Carly's grandmother? I think she was in a Jewish death camp! And then there's Joey's uncle. He's really rich now, but he came over here with no money from Italy after the war!"

"Sounds great to me," replied Evron. "Just don't put your teacher, Mr. Sobalsky, out of a job," he laughed.

The next day, Mr. Sobalsky heard Matt's idea and thought it was worthwhile asking the class to see how much interest there was. Within fifteen minutes, the students had come up with nine more possible guest speakers who were either relatives or people they knew. And Mr. Sobalsky was not worried about his job.

"I think this is wonderful," he told the class. "As young people, it's very important for you to understand what has happened before you were born. It gives you a greater appreciation for what you have now. Interacting with older generations gives you a sense of unity with the past. And you get to meet some new older friends along the way."

When Matt got home that night and told Evron what Mr. Sobalsky had said, Evron replied with a smile, "I couldn't have said it better myself."

A Time for Evron

"It's not the end of the world, you know,"
Matt continued, trying to cheer his friend up.

CHAPTER SIXTEEN

BASKETBALL FEVER

THE LATE FALL SEASON ALSO SIGNALED a special time in Matthew's life - basketball. He loved basketball and looked forward to it each new school year. This year, however, there was one major change. There was going to be only one team from his school area, rather than the usual two. Many of the boys were upset because that meant there would be only half the number of eligible players from his area. There would also be more pressure during tryouts as to who would make the team. Then too, there were many new students in the school, like Richard, who also wanted to try out.

Matthew and Richard talked only about basketball that whole weekend. Tryouts were starting Monday after school and they were trying to get themselves "psyched up". David, a friend of Matthew's who attended another school nearby, telephoned him that Sunday.

"Hi Matt, it's David."

"Hi Dave, long time no see! How's school been going?"

"Great Matt. How about you? I saw your picture in the paper - you've become quite the famous environmentalist. Congratulations."

"Thanks Dave."

"I guess we're going to be competing against each other tomorrow in the tryouts," David continued.

"Yeah, with only one team this year, there are going to be lots of hopefuls who aren't going to make it."

"Well, I just phoned to wish you good luck. I'm sure I'll see you tomorrow."

"Thanks for calling, Dave," Matt replied, "and the best of luck to you too!"

The next afternoon, after school, Richard and Matthew arrived for the tryouts about four p.m.. As they walked into the gym, their mouths dropped. There were at least one hundred boys bouncing balls and practicing drills.

"Oh boy," said Richard, "and they're only going to choose about fifteen of us!"

"Well, " said Matt jokingly, "it's obviously every man for himself. Hey, there's David. C'mon over. I want you to meet him."

Richard and Matt walked over to Dave.

"Hi Dave."

"Hi Matt."

"Dave, I'd like you to meet my new friend at school this year; this is Richard."

"Hi Richard, nice to meet you," Dave said as he puffed for breath.

"Nice to meet you too, Dave," Richard replied. "Wow, are you ever tall! You must be close to six feet."

"Not that tall, Richard, but I'm still growing," Dave smiled back.

"Your height will sure help you in the tryouts."

"I'm not so sure; there are a lot of good players here."

The tryouts continued every afternoon after school. There were also three early morning practices beginning at seven a.m.. Friday's afternoon practice was going to be for only fifteen players. The new team list of those who were successful was to be posted at three-thirty p.m.. Tension was high all day as the boys dreaded going to read the list. Richard and Matt ran over to the gym as soon as they could get out of class. There were already many boys there. Some very happy; some looked very sad. Their hearts were in their mouths as they scanned the list.

"Yeow! We made it!" Matt screamed.

"Whoopee!" yelled Richard, as they gave each other high fives.

They were delirious with excitement as they talked to the others around them. Suddenly Matt said, "Oh, oh, I didn't see Dave's name on the list." He ran back to double check. Sure enough, Dave hadn't made the team.

"Dave will be pretty upset," he was saying to Richard, as he spotted David sitting on the bleachers, his head in his hands.

Both boys walked slowly over to the slumping figure.

"I'm really sorry, Dave," Matt said.

"Me too," added Richard.

David looked up, his eyes red. He had obviously been crying. "I gave it my best guys, what can I say? Congrats to both of you though. I saw your names on the list."

"It's not the end of the world, you know," Matt continued, trying to cheer his friend up.

"That's easy for you to say, Matt, but you don't know my dad that well. He won't accept any excuses."

"Oh he probably won't be that bad," continued Richard, trying to perk him up.

"Oh he will be that bad, believe me. I don't even want to go home. He'll rant and rave all weekend."

"Tell you what," said Matt, "if you can manage to stay for our practice, why not come home afterward to my house for a barbeque. It will be just you and Richard and I. It'll take your mind off everything."

"Thanks Matt, that would be great - anything to delay Dad's anger. Maybe he'll be in bed by the time I get home." David tried to force a smile.

After practice, the three boys walked home quietly together. Although Richard and Matt were still overjoyed about making the team, they didn't want to upset David by being too ecstatic. They knew how upset he was.

Matt put on some of Dave's favorite CD's as he prepared the barbeque on the back porch. No matter how hard he and Richard tried to cheer him up, Dave just seemed very depressed.

"Sorry I'm no fun tonight, guys. I shouldn't have come; I'm spoiling your fun."

"No way!" replied Matt. "You have every right to be down."

Just then Evron came through the patio door. He had been napping in Matt's room.

"Hey Dave, you remember Evron?"

"Sure," Dave replied. "How are you doin' old boy?"

"Actually Dave, you've never really met the real Evron. I think maybe it's time for you to meet the 'real wise one'," Matt laughed quietly. "Evron could you please take Dave inside for a few minutes? He really needs someone to talk to."

"Sure thing, Matt," Evron replied.

Once David got over his initial shock at the talking dog, he and Evron chatted like old friends. David was so happy to talk to someone who was impartial and not personally connected to his life.

"My father thinks, because I'm almost six feet tall and look like Michael Jordan, that I'm supposed to be a basketball star like him. He also says blacks are better basketball players than whites."

"Do you believe that?" asked Evron.

"Not really," responded David. "And you know what, Evron? I don't really care."

"You don't?"

"No, and you know what else, Evron? Between you and me, I don't really even like basketball that much. It's a great sport and all that, but I'm not nuts about it like a lot of my friends. Matt, as an example, lives for it. I don't."

"Do others know this, David?"

"No, I've told no one, not even Matt."

"Why do it then?"

"I guess because everyone thinks I should. Because I'm tall and black, they think I should be a great player. I think deep down I'm afraid of losing my friends if I don't."

"What about your dad?"

"I do it to please him too; that's for sure."

"Why, David?"

"Because he expects it, I guess."

"Are you ever afraid that you might lose his love if you don't do it?" Evron asked.

David was quiet for a moment. "You know Evron, I've never really thought of it like that, but I think you're right. I'm worried that if I don't please him, he'll pull back from me and maybe not love me as much. He sure acts stupidly at times, but I want him to love me."

"Are there any sports you do like?"

"Honestly, Evron, not really. I don't mind a good game of tennis. You know, singles, one to one, but I'm not crazy about team sports. You know what I hate the most? Early morning practices. I'd rather sleep in, than be in some cold gym dribbling a ball at seven in the morning. Boy, I'm talking too much, Evron."

"No, please continue. It's good for you to vent your feelings."

"Well, I guess I've got a lot built up inside me and it's good to get it off my chest. You know something else I don't really care for, Evron?"

"What's that?"

"I can't stand all the 'rah, rah, rah, the team must pull together stuff, being one of the boys,' and all that. I've got nothing against it for others, but I know it's just not me."

"What do you like doing?"

"I'd rather be alone with a good book, or go to a movie or live theater. I love plays and all that. I've even tried writing some short stories."

"You have? Well, have you shown them to anyone?"

"Oh gosh no! I'm afraid I'd be branded a 'wussie' or something."

"But this is what you are happiest doing?"

"Yeah, and I have to hide it."

Evron thought quietly for a moment, then continued, "I think what often happens to young people, David, is that they're searching for who they are and their own sense of self. Because they're often insecure in their own evaluation of themselves, they depend on the approval of their friends and other group members for security. It takes a strong person to stand up for his own beliefs and interests. And when you're very young, it's even harder."

"I think you're right, Evron. It's easier for me to play basketball and please everyone, than to do something that I think isn't acceptable to others."

"Exactly," continued Evron, "but not only that; there are also adult social expectations that may give young people the wrong direction as well."

"How do you mean?"

"Well, look at your own father's comment that blacks make

better basketball players than whites. That really is a racist comment. He's really saying whites are not as good as blacks in sports. Some adults will say that whites are more intelligent than blacks. That too is a racist comment which has never been proven to be true."

"I'm beginning to see what you mean, Evron."

"We dealt with this same thing with David who's Jewish," Evron continued.

"How was that?"

"Well, some of the kids at school said a Jew shouldn't be a truck driver. They were talking about his father."

"What did they think he should be?"

"Oh they thought he should be a doctor, a lawyer, or a movie producer."

"I would never think that," continued David.

"Well, that's because you haven't been exposed to that particular prejudice yet. But, in your own way, you've been exposed to black prejudice."

"So Evron," asked Dave, "help me out here; what am I supposed to do about all this?"

Evron continued. "First of all, just be yourself. Be comfortable with your feelings and be proud of them. If you're not into popular sports, for example basketball, then so be it. Forget it. If others around you don't agree, just smile and say, 'I'm sorry, but I have my own goals and expectations for myself that I'm trying to pursue. Thanks for your thoughts and advice, but I want to work things out for myself.'"

"Wow, I don't know if I'm that secure."

"It's hard at first, but slowly you'll gain more confidence. Actually we all have to struggle to be ourselves, even as adults. And something else, David; in some ways, not making the team is a good thing for you. It's forced you to really look at your situation and perhaps go in a different direction, say with your writing. So it's really been a 'blessing in disguise' as they say."

Dave sighed and sat quietly for a moment. Finally he said, "Well, Evron, thanks for your time. I've talked my head off, but, boy, you can really talk too. You know what though? I honestly feel a whole lot better. I think I'll go home tonight and say to my father, 'Dad, I didn't make the team, but it's not the end of the world. It'll give me more time to write. By the way Dad, I'd like you to read some of my stories.'"

"That sounds wonderful to me," responded Evron, "and by the way, David, could I read a few too?"

"For sure!" he replied. "Now let's go out and help our basketball stars with the barbeque."

A Time for Evron

Richard's dad drove them to the restaurant the next evening and, after their pizza, they walked over to the theater. The line up at six fifteen was already getting long and many of the kids from school were excitedly waiting to get in.

CHAPTER SEVENTEEN

A NEW NEIGHBOR

SATURDAY MORNINGS during the school year were a very quiet time for Matthew. He usually slept in until nine or ten o'clock and then watched some cartoons on T.V.. Then he had his chores to do. These included such tasks as cleaning up the kitchen and the bathrooms as well as vacuuming. As usual, his dad had left much earlier for work. Because of the new service station, his father wasn't home as much now, and Matthew was expected to do more around the house.

He had just finished scrubbing down the bathtub when he heard the telephone ring. It was Mrs. Spencer from next door. Matt liked Mr. and Mrs. Spencer as neighbors, but didn't see or talk to them very much because they had no kids his age. They had one daughter who was grown up, had married and moved away.

"Good morning, Matthew, how have you been?" asked Mrs. Spencer.

"Fine," replied Matthew; "I'm just finishing up my chores."

"Oh that's great," she continued. "It's nice of you to help your dad out so much. By the way, I have a young visitor from out West whom I would like you to meet. I wondered if I could bring her over and introduce her."

"Why, sure," answered Matthew.

"She's my niece and she's going to be living with Mr. Spencer and me from now on. Nadja is about your age."

"Oh," continued Matthew, somewhat surprised.

"I'll be enrolling her in school on Monday. I guess she'll be in your class."

"Probably. Come on over when you're ready, Mrs. Spencer."

Matthew hung up the phone. He was slightly worried. "Guess what, Evron? Mrs. Spencer is going to bring her niece over to meet me. She's going to move in with them and go to my school. I think she wants me to be her friend. A girl is the last thing I need in my life right now. I'll have to introduce her to Sylvie."

"Don't panic," replied Evron. "Her aunt is probably just trying to make her feel at home and meet someone her own age. How would you feel if you were new to a neighborhood?"

"Oh, don't worry; I'll be nice to her. I just can't wait till she starts school on Monday and meets other kids."

Before long, the doorbell rang and Mrs. Spencer appeared with the new girl in town. "Good morning Matthew; I'd like you to meet Nadja."

"Hi Nadja," replied Matthew; "please come in, both of you."

"Nice to meet you," said Nadja quietly.

At times like this, Matthew felt awkward. His mom or dad were much better at making people feel at home, but, of course, neither of them was around.

"Please come in and sit down in the living room. This is my dog, Evron."

"Oh he's so cute," replied Nadja as Evron wagged his tail.

Matthew made some tea for Mrs. Spencer while he and Nadja had some pop and chips.

"If you're not too busy today, Matthew, I wondered if you could perhaps take Nadja down and show her the park?" asked Mrs. Spencer, hopefully.

A Time for Evron

"Sure thing," answered Matthew. "Maybe there will be some baseball games on this afternoon and perhaps we could play some tennis. If this warm weather continues, everyone will keep playing summer games."

"I'd like that," replied Nadja. "I used to play some tennis at home."

"Great then!" continued Matthew. "I'll bring over the racquets and balls and meet you in half an hour at your house."

"That would be wonderful, Matthew," smiled Mrs. Spencer.

After Nadja and her aunt left, Matthew said, "Oh well, Evron, there goes the afternoon. Richard and I were going to go on a bicycle hike today."

"Oh, ... it's not that bad," kidded Evron. "You're doing something nice for somebody. Besides Nadja will find new girlfriends next week when she starts school. This inconvenience won't last long."

"I sure hope not," replied Matt.

It wasn't long before Matt and Evron and Nadja were on their way to the park. Matt had brought Evron's ball so he could play "fetch". Evron hated this doggie game, but he had to play the part of a real dog at times and anyway it was good exercise for him.

There were three tennis courts in the park and none were being used. Matt and Nadja hit the ball back and forth for about an hour and Evron retrieved the balls that went over the fence. It didn't take long for them to get very tired. There was a pop machine beside the courts and Matt bought Nadja a Coke. They sat down on a bench to rest as they sipped their drinks. Evron sat in the shade nearby. "Thanks for bringing me down here today," said Nadja. "I'm sure you had other things you would rather have been doing."

"Oh, that's okay," replied Matt. "I'm glad to be able to

show you around. You must feel sort of lost in a new town and everything."

"I think I'm feeling lost in general, Matt. My mom died this past week and there have been lots of family problems."

"Oh gosh," stammered Matt. "I'm so sorry; I had no idea. Your aunt didn't say why you were here."

"That's okay. Aunt Sarah said she thought it was better if I decided when and how to tell people myself. My mom died of cancer and we kids weren't told she had it until three weeks ago."

"Who are the other kids?" Matt asked.

"I have two younger brothers. Each of us had to go and live with a different aunt because no one was able to take us all together. They're still out West."

"Wow!" sighed Matt, suddenly feeling guilty that he had been so selfish in not wanting to spend some time with Nadja.

Evron appeared to be snoozing nearby, but of course was listening intently to everything.

"If you don't mind my asking," inquired Matt, "where is your father?"

Nadja was silent for a short time, then she replied. "He's very sick. He wasn't able to keep the family together after Mom died."

Matt didn't know what to say next. Nadja didn't seem to want to talk about it anymore; so he changed the subject. "Well, let's go for a walk and I'll show you the river and some of the other exciting highlights of our town," he said laughingly as he tried to cheer her up.

Later that night, when he got into bed, he said to Evron.

"Remember that night I got you for my birthday, Evron, and I was crying because Mom and Amy were no longer living with me and dad?"

A Time for Evron

"Yes, I do," replied Evron. "I remember it well; it's the first time I spoke to you."

"Well," continued Matt, "I'm thinking of how sad I was then. Now I'm trying to imagine how sad Nadja must feel. Her mom is dead and her father and brothers are all separated from her too. I feel so badly for her."

"Yes, it's very tragic," answered Evron. "It makes you realize sometimes that no matter how bad you may think your own life is, someone else is worse off."

"Well, I'm going to try and make her as happy as I can," replied Matthew, perking up.

"I'm sure you will," answered Evron and they hugged each other good night.

Mrs. Spencer had told Matthew that she and Mr. Spencer were going to take Nadja out for a drive on Sunday to show her some of the countryside. She said they would drop into the service centre for gasoline and introduce Nadja to Matt's dad as well.

After dinner on Sunday, Matthew and Evron dropped into the Spencer's house to see how everything was going. "I brought you some workbooks and a binder, Nadja," Matt said. "All the students in my class use these basically for taking notes."

"That's wonderful; thank you. I think I'll have enough to worry about tomorrow without having to think about getting workbooks too."

"I know you're a bit nervous, but don't worry. Mr. Sobalsky is very nice and he'll make you feel comfortable."

The next morning, Mrs. Spencer drove Nadja to school to register her with Mr. Evans, the principal. Matthew waited anxiously during the morning class period. He knew Mr. Evans would be bringing Nadja down shortly to introduce her to the students.

There was soon a knock on the door and in walked Nadja.

Matthew felt so upset for her that his heart was pounding. He had already spoken to Mr. Sobalsky about Nadja coming from out West and Richard had agreed to give up his seat beside Matt so that Nadja could sit there.

Mr. Evans was speaking. "Good morning, class; I would like to introduce you to Nadja who has just arrived from the west coast. It's difficult to change schools part way through the year, but I know you will all make her feel welcome here in her new class."

Nadja sat down shyly beside Matthew and gave him a big smile. "I'm so nervous, Matt," she whispered.

"You'll be just fine," he grinned back and touched her arm gently. The morning class went on as usual, with boardwork to copy down, some class discussions, and then a homework assignment.

At recess time, Matthew introduced Nadja to Richard and Sylvie. Sylvie said that she would introduce her to more of the girls outside in the school yard. As Matthew saw Nadja run off with Sylvie, he felt somewhat relieved that someone else was taking care of her. "I'm glad she'll meet some girlfriends now," he said as he winked at Richard.

That afternoon after school, Matt had hoped that Sylvie would walk Nadja home; however, she had band practice so he and Richard decided to show her the sights in town instead: the local post office, movie theatre, variety store, snack bars and, of course, Sylvie's mom's store. Matthew thought it was great having Richard along because he didn't have to worry continually about keeping the conversation going. Nadja was still very quiet at times. At one time, when Nadja was talking to Richard, Matthew was quietly looking at her. He couldn't help noticing her big blue eyes and pretty smile.

By Friday, Nadja was part of the regular group walking home

with Matthew, Richard, and Sylvie. As they all chatted, Sylvie said, "I have a great idea; why don't we all go to a movie tomorrow?"

"Why not?" replied Richard. "There's a new horror movie at the Roxy this weekend."

"Sounds great! Let's go for pizza first and then catch the seven o'clock show," exclaimed Matt.

"That sounds like fun. I'm sure Aunt Sarah will let me go," Nadja replied, excitedly.

Richard's dad drove them to the restaurant the next evening and, after their pizza, they walked over to the theater. The line up at six-fifteen was already getting long and many of the kids from school were excitedly waiting to get in. After half an hour, they finally got to the ticket wicket and into the theater. Richard and Matthew treated the girls to popcorn and milkshakes and then the four of them rushed to get good seats. Everyone liked sitting close to the front. Being gentlemanly, the boys let the girls into the row first and then they followed. Matthew ended up sitting beside Nadja. "I hope this movie isn't too scary," she said.

"Don't worry; we'll protect you," Matthew joked.

The movie was very frightening at times, but the audience loved it. There was lots of screaming. In one really scary scene, Nadja grabbed Matt's hand hard and screamed so loudly that his ears hurt. He couldn't help but laugh at her being so frightened. As the movie continued, Nadja kept her hand in Matthew's. He was surprised at first and then quickly decided he liked holding her hand. As everyone filed out of the theater after the movie was over, they let their hands go and acted as though nothing had happened. Nadja's aunt was there to meet them and take them all home.

That night in his room, Matthew and Evron talked. "I really liked holding her hand, Evron. I also just like being with her."

"Well that's really great that you enjoy each other," replied Evron.

"I think about her a lot now. I can't seem to get her out of my mind. I don't know whether it's because I feel sorry for her and want to protect her or what it is. You're probably going to say it's puppy love again, like with Jessica."

"Maybe so," replied Evron, "but friendships and emotional involvement with others are very complicated. No two relationships are the same."

"So what should I do about her?" asked Matthew.

"Just carry on as you are doing," answered Evron. "Just take it a day at a time."

That week, Matthew asked Nadja if she would like to go to the movies again, but this time just the two of them. Nadja excitedly said 'yes'.

That night at the movies, they held hands again. At one point, Nadja even put her head on Matt's shoulder. Because it was a warm night, they walked home and didn't need a ride. This time they continued holding hands. Matthew was very happy. He said, "You know, Nadja, I feel I've known you for a long, long time and yet, it's only been a couple of weeks."

"Me too," she replied. "I'm very happy being with you."

As they approached her front door, Matthew said, "thanks for a wonderful evening; I really had fun."

"I've really enjoyed it too," Nadja replied shyly.

Matt then leaned forward and kissed her on the cheek. She kissed him back. His heart was pounding. "Well, goodnight," he stammered.

"Goodnight Matt; and thanks again. I'll see you at school on Monday."

Matt couldn't wait for Monday to see Nadja again. He could hardly stop sneaking glances at her all day in class and was excited that she and Richard and he were walking home together that afternoon.

A Time for Evron

But after school, Nadja said, "Sylvie and I are going to her mom's store this afternoon, and then she's taking us out for dinner."

"Oh ... oh, that's okay, maybe tomorrow then," replied Matt, somewhat disappointed.

That night at home he said to Evron, "I'm hurt that they didn't invite Richard and me to go along with them."

"I don't think this is serious enough to get hurt over," replied Evron. "Don't forget, Nadja has other friends and interests besides you. You don't have to be with her all the time."

"Oh, I know that," answered Matthew.

"I think maybe you're a little jealous of someone else being with Nadja, aren't you?" asked Evron.

"I guess ... I guess I am a bit."

For the rest of the week, Matthew thought Nadja seemed less excited about being around him and Richard. She was polite and everything, but she seemed to want to hang out more with Sylvie and the other girls. That Friday, he finally got the nerve to say to her, "Richard and I wondered if you and Sylvie wanted to go to the roller derby this weekend?"

"That sounds like fun, Matt; I'll ask Sylvie after school and let you know. I'll meet you at your locker," Nadja replied.

"That's great, see you then."

After school, he eagerly waited for her by his locker. He smiled broadly as he spotted her down the hallway, walking towards him.

"Hi Matthew, thanks for asking us to the roller derby, but Sylvie and I and some of the other girls want to go on our own, if you don't mind. Sort of 'a girls night out; no boys allowed,' if that's okay with you. We'll look for you guys there."

"Oh ... well, okay," sighed Matthew. "I just thought it would be nice if we could all go together like at the movies."

"You know, Matthew, I've been thinking about us,"

replied Nadja, "and I've talked it over with Aunt Sarah." She took a deep breath. "You and I have become good friends and I like you very much, but I think we saw too much of each other too soon."

"Why?" asked Matt, really shocked.

"Well, it's just that I'd rather spend more time with my girl-friends right now then be tied down with a boyfriend."

"It's not exactly like that," gulped Matt.

"You know what I mean, Matt," she replied. "We just need some time away from each other. You've been wonderful to me and really helped me feel welcome here. I appreciate that."

"I understand, and you're right. I guess I became a little suf-focating," he joked and tried to force a smile. "Thanks for being honest with me."

"Thanks for being understanding, Matthew. Maybe we'll see you tomorrow at the derby." Then she ran off to greet Sylvie down the hallway.

Matthew walked home quietly, thinking about his talk with Nadja. As soon as he came through the door, Evron knew some-thing was wrong. "It's Nadja, isn't it?" asked Evron.

"Yes," replied Matthew, almost in tears, and told Evron the whole story.

"These hurt feelings are a part of life," replied Evron. "Relationships with others are very complex. You cared for Nadja and worried about her and eventually developed a crush on her. This is only natural. Unfortunately, she doesn't have a crush on you."

"So what can I do?" asked Matthew.

"Nothing. Be as friendly and polite to her as you would be to anyone else. Keep all the other interests and friends that you had before she came along. You were fine then. In time, you won't feel so badly."

"Well, I guess I better start right now," perked up Matthew. "I've got to get dinner ready for dad and take it to him at the station."

Evron smiled quietly and thought to himself, "Matthew will adapt to his new situation just fine."

"I don't like talking about my problems much, Evron, because I'm afraid others won't understand or won't care."

CHAPTER EIGHTEEN

SEPARATION AND LOSS

MATTHEW DID SLOWLY ADAPT to his new relationship with Nadja. They still sat beside each other in class and they were still friends - but there wasn't that close intensity he had felt earlier. Actually, he realized that in many ways, it was better. He was more relaxed and could spend more time with his boyfriends.

Two weeks before Christmas, his class was involved one afternoon in putting up decorations and getting into the Christmas spirit. Students were all over the room. Some were climbing ladders to hang lights from the ceiling; others were taping decorations on the windows and doors. Some were practicing a sing-song in one corner while another group was rehearsing for the Christmas play.

As Matt rushed by Nadja on his way to get some decorations, he noticed that she was crying - just standing there in the middle of the room, quietly crying. No one else had even noticed. "What's wrong?" he asked quietly as he leaned close to her.

"Nothing really," she replied. "I just don't feel very good. Do you think Mr. Sobalsky will let me go home?"

"I'll ask him if we can both leave and I'll walk with you. Come over to his desk with me," whispered Matthew.

Mr. Sobalsky said they would have to ask permission from the office; so Nadja and Matthew left the room to see Mr. Evans. The principal's receptionist telephoned Nadja's aunt at work, and Matt's dad at the service centre, for permission, and before long they were on their way home.

"Seeing everyone have so much fun today in class made me realize how much I miss my home and brothers," Nadja cried quietly. "I like my aunt and uncle and everyone here, Matthew, but I really miss my mom."

Matthew was at a loss for words. "I'm upset for you," he replied. "I wish I could make you happier; I just don't know what to do."

"My sadness comes and goes," continued Nadja. "I guess today is just a bad day."

"Are you going home for Christmas?" asked Matt.

"No, my aunt and uncle can't afford the airfare this year."

"What about your dad paying?" Matt asked.

"My father has no job right now, Matthew. He's also an alcoholic and it's hard for alcoholics to find work."

"Oh boy," sighed Matt. "I'm sorry I asked, Nadja; I really didn't mean to be nosy."

"That's alright. Sometimes I'm ashamed of him and don't want anyone to know and then sometimes I don't care."

"When you said he was sick earlier, was it the alcoholism you meant?"

"Yes. With his drinking, he's incapable of taking care of the three of us. Sometimes he spends his unemployment check on booze, so there's very little money left for food or clothing or rent."

"Has he ever tried to stop his drinking?"

"Yes, he has for a while, but then he starts up again."

"How did he feel when you three kids had to leave him?" asked Matthew.

A Time for Evron

"Actually, I think he was relieved. Then he didn't have to worry about us. You see my mother did all the worrying before."

"But he must miss his own kids."

"Oh, I guess he does in his own way, Matt, but not enough to give up his alcohol to keep us. He would rather have his booze." They walked in silence for a while.

As they approached Nadja's house, Matthew spoke softly: "Would you like to come to my place for some juice and a snack?"

"No ... thanks anyway, but I think I'd just like to go home and have a nap. I'm feeling quite tired."

"Alright then, hopefully you'll feel better tomorrow. Bye for now."

Matthew felt pretty upset as he arrived home. Evron was surprised to see him out of school so early. "Nadja's so upset. If only I could do something for her."

Then Matt told Evron the latest developments in Nadja's story.

"Let's go over to her house and you can introduce her to me," said Evron.

"She knows you already," replied Matt.

"No, I mean as the real me Matt, not just the cute little dog."

"Why?" Matt asked.

"Well, I think she can probably use a furry shoulder to cry on. You can ask her aunt if I can stay with her tonight to keep her company."

"Alright then, we'll give it a try."

Like everybody else when they first discovered Evron could talk, Nadja was in shock. "I've always wanted a dog, but was never allowed one because we lived in an apartment. I never thought I'd see a talking dog though," she smiled as she and Matt and Evron sat together.

"Do you think your Aunt Sarah will let Evron stay with you tonight?"

"For sure! They have been talking about getting me a dog anyway!"

"That's great then," Matt continued.

"We'll just say Evron is a tryout to see how a dog works," she laughed.

Matt hadn't seen her laugh in a long time.

Later that day, Aunt Sarah thought it was wonderful that Matt let Evron stay with Nadja for a while.

In the evening, with Evron in her room, Nadja was still very shy with him as they talked together on Nadja's new bed which her aunt had bought her. "I don't like talking about my problems much, Evron, because I'm afraid others won't understand or won't care. I don't know any other kid whose mother has died or whose father is an alcoholic; so how could they possibly understand how I feel?"

"Well there are lots of kids out there with alcoholic parents, but, like you Nadja, they just don't talk about it. There actually are many support groups in communities for alcoholics and their families."

"There are?"

"Yes. For instance, there are groups called Alanon for children and spouses of alcoholics. These are people who have experiences similar to yours. You act as support for each other."

"It would be great to talk to others who understand me. I feel so alone some times."

"And there are also bereavement groups, Nadja."

"What's a bereavement group?"

"It's a group for people who have lost someone, very close to them - perhaps a mother, a father a brother or a sister. All group members share their feelings."

"I'm not sure I could talk to a group about my mom."

"That's fine," continued Evron; "they are not for everyone,

but you might think of trying it out to see if it helps."

"Do you think there is one at my school?"

"Probably."

"But I haven't heard anyone mention it."

"Don't forget, Nadja; you haven't told anyone except Matt about your mother. People wouldn't suggest it unless they knew about her death."

"That's true." She was quiet for awhile with her eyes closed; then she whispered, "Do you believe in heaven, Evron? Do you think my mom is there?"

Evron was very still for a few moments, then replied, "I'm not certain about heaven, Nadja, but I do believe in the human spirit or the human soul."

"What is that?"

"Well, I think that the body has an energy within it. It's basically an energy to love and a need to be loved. We can't see the energy, but we can feel it. We feel it in ourselves and we feel it in others."

"Does it die when we die?" she asked.

"I think when we die, our soul leaves our bodies and exits into the universe."

"Does the soul ever return to Earth?"

"I think the soul travels back and forth everywhere, Nadja."

"Sometimes I feel that my mom is right here with me, Evron."

"That's quite possible. Perhaps her soul is with you!"

"Are these souls a part of your planet also, Evron?"

"I believe they are; I believe they are wherever there is life in the universe."

"I sometimes talk to my mom at night, Evron. Sometimes I cry when I'm alone because I miss her so much. I feel so lonely at times."

"It's natural for you to be upset, Nadja. There are many hurts and losses we sometimes have to work out alone. But don't forget one thing; there are others here to support you."

"But do you think she hears me?"

"I'm certain she does, Nadja; she is here for you."

Nadja looked at Evron and smiled. "Thank you for staying with me tonight. It's great having you to talk to."

"You're a very sensitive girl, Nadja. It will take a while, but you'll start to feel better gradually."

"I guess so Evron. Will you do me a favor?"

"Anything that I can, Nadja," he replied.

"Come over here and cuddle with me while I sleep."

Evron moved closer to Nadja. She put her arms around him and lay her head peacefully on her pillow and slept.

A Time for Evron

"The hardest part is never knowing when the shooting will start."

CHAPTER NINETEEN

WORLDWIDE TERROR

ACCOMPANIED BY HER AUNT AND UNCLE for support, Nadja began to take some counseling very soon. One of the things Evron also wanted her to do was to get involved in some activity which would keep her distracted from her own troubles while, at the same time, helping others.

Nadja had seen the advertisements on television for "Save the Children" and decided that she would initiate a campaign at school for these less fortunate children. Her goal was to get as many students as possible each to sponsor a child in an impoverished country. Mr. Sobalsky asked for volunteers from the class to help Nadja with the project. Along with Richard and Matt, a new boy to the school, named Vahid, offered to help her.

Nadja arranged for their first meeting to take place after school in the library. Richard, Matthew and Nadja were eager to get to know Vahid better and to make him feel welcome in their new group.

"I am from Azerbaijan which was a republic of the former Soviet Union," Vahid declared. "My mother and I are here now just this summer. My older brother and sister are still there. We are hoping they will get out next summer."

"Why didn't you all come over together?" asked Nadja.

"We have little money; so we couldn't all leave at once."

"Do you have relatives here in this country?" inquired Richard.

"Oh, no, but this was a free country that was accepting refugees," answered Vahid.

"So why did you leave your country?" asked Matt.

"There are terrible wars over there," choked Vahid; "everyone is trying to kill each other. Russia is trying to conquer us."

"I guess we don't hear much about it over here," said Richard.

"You are right. Because my country is so far away, there is no interest here."

"It must seem as if we're talking only about you at this meeting," said Nadja. "We don't mean to centre you out, Vahid, but none of us have ever experienced these types of problems and we're interested."

"It's been pretty bad back home for a long time. We often have no food or water and there is no heat or electricity."

Everyone was quiet for a moment; then Vahid continued, "The hardest part is never knowing when the shooting will start. It can be quiet for a few days and then they are suddenly shooting their guns at you. It could be during the day or night."

"Who are they?" asked Matt.

"The Russian troops," answered Vahid.

"How do you go to school?" asked Nadja.

"Sometimes you don't go to school for weeks and weeks," said Vahid, sounding very upset. "Other times, they even shoot at the schools."

"I guess you might get killed if you were out in the open for long," Richard commented.

"Did you ever know anyone who was killed?" asked Matt.

Vahid looked at the group for a moment; then he replied,

"My dad was killed." He started to cry silently.

In response, Nadja started to cry and Richard and Matthew both had tears in their eyes. Nadja went over and hugged Vahid. Matt and Richard sat still. No one said anything.

"Maybe we should continue our meeting another time," observed Matt.

"No, no ... I'll be fine," murmured Vahid. "I'm so sorry I upset you."

"Don't be sorry, Vahid. It's important we know these things," said Matt.

"Yeah," agreed Richard, "sometimes we worry too much about ourselves. Maybe it's time we worried more about others."

"I wish more of the world knew of our troubles there," replied Vahid.

"I have a great idea," exclaimed Nadja excitedly. "Why don't we have Vahid give a presentation to the class on Azerbaijan? We can all help him present it so that he doesn't have to do it all by himself."

"Cool," exclaimed Richard. "Then, if we make the class more aware of what is happening there, we will get sponsorship money for kids in Azerbaijan. Because Vahid has lived there and gone through all of these horrors, it makes it more personal for everyone."

"I will be glad to do it," replied Vahid, "as long as you all help me."

"Great," concluded Nadja. "I'll speak to Mr. Sobalsky tomorrow to get his permission. I know he'll think it's a great idea."

That night Matt was at home telling everything to Evron. "I think it's a very good project for all of you, Matthew," he said, "but why not take it a big step further?"

"And do what?" asked Matt. "Here we go again with your ideas," he chuckled.

"Well, let's say Vahid had lots of school friends in his country."

"Okay," replied Matt.

"Then let's also assume that his friend's families are all in difficulty like Vahid's family."

"Right."

"So why not have each student in your class help out at least one student's family in Vahid's class back in Azerbaijan. Let's really personalize this help, Matthew."

Matthew thought quietly for a moment and then said, "That's fine, Evron, but we were not planning on asking the students for a whole lot of money, at least not enough money to help out a whole family."

"Not a whole lot more, Matthew," answered Evron, "but maybe more than they might normally give."

"Perhaps it's too much to ask my friends, and their parents, especially at Christmas time," continued Matt.

"But what if the students were to donate some of the money their parents would spend on them for Christmas to an Azerbaijan family instead?"

"Wow, that might be okay," replied Matt excitedly. "Do you really think they would go for it?"

"Yes, I do. For example, Matt, what is the cost of a present you might get for Christmas?"

"Oh, maybe around twenty-five dollars."

"So if you were to give up that one gift for Christmas, and you took the money instead, you could donate twenty-five dollars to an Azerbaijan family."

"That's right," responded Matt.

"Then what about everyone in the class donating twenty-five dollars from their Christmas money?" asked Evron.

"Well, let's see what they say. Giving up one gift sure doesn't seem very important compared to helping out a family fighting a war."

A Time for Evron

"I think it's also better, Matthew, that each student in your class give up something he or she wants. In this way, their gifts are more personal."

"It's like it's more from the heart," observed Matt.

"Exactly," replied Evron. "There is actually a word for it; it's called 'ALTRUISM', which means 'regard for the interest of others'. At your age, it is time to start developing this quality."

A few days later, Vahid's class presentation was a great success. The four classmates each had a part explaining such things as the weather, businesses and industries of the region and, in a very simple way, the manner in which the country was divided into regions.

Vahid discussed the various nationalities and religions of his country and even had some family photos displayed. Matthew and Richard and Nadja talked about some of the fighting and the people killed. The class was absolutely shocked when they were told of Vahid's father also being killed in a gun battle.

The students were excited about giving up some of their money for Vahid's friends back home. Two of the students in the class were Jewish and three were Muslim and, even though they didn't celebrate Christmas, they wanted to donate as well. Richard said that the most similar Jewish festival was probably Chanukah, and he definitely wanted to be part of the giving spirit.

Mr. Sobalsky helped collect the money from his students and proudly presented it to Vahid's mother. She cried the day of the presentation and, in her broken English, told the class how she had special ways of smuggling the money back to the families in Azerbaijan. She was truly touched that Vahid's new friends half a world away could care so much for his old friends back home.

The first return letters from Azerbaijan began to arrive about six weeks after the holidays. The students eagerly waited each day for Vahid to translate them to the class. Vahid's new classmates were surprised at how the letters could just have easily come from someone living next door, rather than thousands of miles away. The emotions were no different than their own. They were slowly beginning to learn that, with all the freedom and material things which they enjoyed in their country, also came the obligation to care for others who were less fortunate elsewhere.

Vahid came to love and trust his new friends as he never thought he would again.

That evening, during their quiet time together, Evron said, "You see Matthew, all over the world, people are basically the same. Given the chance, they are loving, and giving and caring for others. Nationalities and great distances make no difference."

Just one week later, during a math lesson, Mr. Evans the principal, announced over the public address system that he was calling an assembly in the school auditorium. He sounded upset and sad. Everyone was speculating about the reason for the sudden meeting as the classrooms emptied and hundreds of young people filed into the huge room.

As the students sat quietly on the auditorium floor, two large television monitors were wheeled to the front of the gathering. Mr. Evans approached the front microphone. He spoke somberly, "Except for the youngest pupils, I have gathered you here today to inform you of a shocking terrorist attack on New York City and Washington." He continued to elaborate,outlining the details of the attack and the latest projected casualty figures in the thousands. The monitors were turned on and everyone watched the shocking developments on CNN. Some students gasped at the horrible scenes on the screen, others cried. Mr. Evans then encouraged the teachers to return to their rooms, and "talk out" the terrible events with their students. He wanted his student body to be prepared for the tragic information that would play out on their television screens that evening.

As his kids were returning to their classroom, Mr. Sobalsky observed sullenly, how sad and upset the young people appeared. Only weeks before they had shown the same emotions, during Vahid's startling presentation.

Matthew and his classmates were eager to discuss their anger, feelings of apprehension, and sense of helplessness at this recent tragedy. Images of Mr. Burrows's war presentation months earlier, flooded back into their thoughts. The destruction and terror that Vahid had shown them, only in pictures, was now brought to a shocking reality close to home. Human destruction and acts of war were capable of happening anywhere.

As the young people left school that afternoon, they felt a shock and sadness they had never experienced before.

Adi's head was bowed now as she stared at her hands that were clasped together tightly in her lap. She made no response. Mr. Sobalsky thought how delicate and frightened she appeared.

CHAPTER TWENTY

MONEY PROBLEMS

DURING THE FUNDRAISING FOR AZERBAIJAN, one particular student in the class came to Mr. Sobalsky's attention. He didn't say anything to her at first because he didn't want to embarrass the young girl and he figured there had to be a good reason for her behavior. Her name was Adi and she hadn't contributed any money to the overseas fund. Because he was the money collector, no one knew this except himself and, of course, Adi. He watched her closely during the fundraising campaign and he was certain she had told no one. It was as if she was just like all the other students.

He thought about how to handle this touchy situation for a long while. He finally decided to ask her to stay one afternoon after school and to approach the topic tactfully. He knew that she was very uneasy that day as the last student rushed from the classroom and he and Adi were left alone.

"Please sit down, Adi," Mr. Sobalsky said, as she approached his desk. "I have a few matters I would like to discuss with you. I'm not mad at you or anything, but I do have a few concerns." Adi looked frightened as she stared back at him. Mr. Sobalsky took a deep breath and then continued. "You and I know Adi that you contributed no money to the Azerbaijan fund and I was wondering why?"

Adi's head was bowed now as she stared at her hands that were clasped together tightly in her lap. She made no response. Mr. Sobalsky thought how delicate and frightened she appeared. There was still no response. "Adi?" he continued, "please answer me."

He got up slowly from his desk and walked around to where she was sitting. He crouched down gently so that their faces were close together. Adi's eyes were filled with tears which were dropping slowly into her lap. "Here Adi," offered Mr. Sobalsky, "please take this tissue." She took the tissue, dabbing her eyes slowly. Her frail body shook with broken sobs. Mr. Sobalsky waited quietly until she began to calm down. "Adi, I'm sorry you're so upset, but nothing is going to happen to you. This talk is just between you and me. Please let me know why you're crying."

"I ... I didn't give any money to the fund because ... because we have no money to give. We're very poor. I hate the word, but it's true, we're poor. We don't even have much money for food. I'm upset that I never told Nadja. I feel I've been dishonest with her because she started up the fund."

Mr. Sobalsky sat down quietly beside her. "I'm sorry, Adi; I had no idea. Had I known, I never would have pushed you for an answer to the money question. Does the principal know about your family situation?"

"No, no one knows. I'm very ashamed and I made my mom promise not to tell."

"Where do you live, Adi?" Mr. Sobalsky asked gently.

"We rent a small old farmhouse outside of town."

"Do your parents work?"

"My dad hasn't worked in two years. He stays home with my baby sister while my mom works at a warehouse. I come to school on the school bus."

"You say you don't have enough money for food, Adi?"

"Well, it's hard because we have to spend a lot of money to

heat the house in winter. It's not well insulated and there are cracks in the walls. My dad says that fuel oil is very expensive; he even goes out looking for dead trees and branches to cut up as firewood for our little stove. That way we don't use the furnace as much. We can't even afford pills when we get sick. We can't even afford to take my cat to the veterinarian and she's very sick. I think she might die."

"I'm very sorry, Adi. What's wrong with your cat?"

"She got in a fight and her back leg was torn up. Now it's infected and she can't walk. I'm so worried about her."

"Do you pay much rent?"

"The landlord charges us only three hundred dollars a month which my mom says is pretty good, but it's still hard to keep up with expenses."

Adi started sobbing again and Mr. Sobalsky gave her more tissues. He sighed deeply because he felt so badly for her. He tried to figure out what to do next.

"Adi, do you have any friends at school you can confide in?"

"What does 'confide in' mean?"

"Oh, that means talking to someone in private, someone who would keep your story a secret. It would be better for you to have a young friend you can talk to."

"No, no I can't do that. I'm too ashamed. All these kids have families with lots of money and their lives seem so perfect. They don't want to be bothered with me."

"That's not always true, Adi," continued Mr. Sobalsky; "often, others' lives are not as perfect as they appear." He couldn't help thinking of Nadja and her troubled family.

"Do you ever go on sleepovers with other girls?"

"Oh no, I can't do that because then I would have to have a sleepover at my house in return. My house is so junky; I'd be too embarrassed for them to see it."

Mr. Sobalsky fell silent again and was wondering how he was going to help Adi. She had mentioned Nadja earlier, and how she felt she had been dishonest with her. He now thought he would try exploring this angle.

"Do you like Nadja?" he asked.

"Nadja? Oh yes, she seems nice, but I don't speak to her much. She has her own group of friends."

Mr. Sobalsky never spoke of personal problems of one student to another, but he was now thinking of all Nadja's personal difficulties of which he had become aware as her teacher. Nadja's Aunt Sarah, and Nadja herself, had spoken to him about her family problems and of her need, at times, to miss school for counseling sessions. Mr. Sobalsky had been impressed with Nadja's sensitivity and her determination to begin feeling better about herself. He felt certain she would be a caring young person to listen to Adi's problems.

He then continued, "How would you feel about telling Nadja why you didn't give money to the 'Save the Children Fund'?"

"Oh gosh, do you think she would be mad at me, Mr. Sobalsky?"

"No, Adi, I don't; I think she would be very understanding of your problem. I think she would be upset for you."

"You do?"

"Yes, Nadja's very sensitive to the feelings of others, Adi."

"It sure would be nice to talk to someone my age about my problems."

"Maybe Nadja could be the one," replied Mr. Sobalsky.

"That would be wonderful," Adi continued.

"With your permission then, Adi, I will speak to her and see how she feels about the three of us meeting. You can talk to her about as much or as little as you want."

"Well, I guess we can give it a try, Mr. Sobalsky. I even feel a bit better now after talking to you."

A Time for Evron

"Thanks for trusting me, Adi. I don't think that Nadja will disappoint you. Provided she has the time and agrees, we three will meet here tomorrow after school. Okay?"

"Okay then," replied Adi, "and thanks for caring so much, Mr. Sobalsky. I have to catch my bus now."

As Adi left the room, Mr. Sobalsky was glad to see that she was at least talking to someone about her problems. He was still worried though about how she could be helped.

The next day, he approached Nadja at recess about talking to him and Adi for a few minutes after school. "I'll try to do anything I can for her," Nadja said enthusiastically.

Later that afternoon, the three met privately in the classroom. "Thanks for coming this afternoon, Nadja." began Mr. Sobalsky. "Adi and I have some things we'd like to share with you."

Nadja sat in silence as Adi told her about her problems and not having any money to donate to the fund. She looked into Adi's eyes and recognized the hurt and the pain. "Is your father a drinker?" Nadja asked calmly.

"A drinker?" replied Adi, not understanding the question.

"Yes, does he drink a lot of beer, or wine, or alcohol?"

"Gosh no, we hardly have enough money for food and certainly no money for that stuff."

"Well, lack of food never stopped my father from drinking," Nadja shot back without thinking and then wished she hadn't responded so harshly.

"But, you're not poor, Nadja. I've seen how you dress and everything."

"That's because I live with my aunt and uncle now, Adi. But I sure was poor when I lived out West with my real family."

Nadja quickly summarized her family story for Adi. Even Mr. Sobalsky was surprised at some of the sad details involving her father and his drinking. When she was finished, Adi spoke qui-

141

etly. "I'm sorry, Nadja; I never would have guessed. You seem so normal and happy now."

"I try to be, but I still have a lot of anger and hurt inside."

"That's how I feel!" replied Adi. "Anger - that's a good way to describe it, Nadja. I'm mad that I'm poor, mad my dad doesn't have a job, mad my cat is sick and I can't help her and I'm mad I couldn't give money to your fundraiser." She started to cry. Nadja went up to her and hugged her. She didn't let go as Adi continued to sob, her head on Nadja's shoulder. "Listen," Nadja said gently, "I'd love for you to come and stay at my house this weekend. You'll love my aunt and uncle and we'll have a 'girls weekend'."

"That sounds cool," smiled Adi, "but you'll have to tell me what to bring; I've never been to a sleepover before."

Mr. Sobalsky was pleased that both girls were obviously getting along well; they had more in common than even he had realized. He worried though that those so young in age had already been through so much unhappiness.

A Time for Evron

"She sure is very sick," he said with a big frown. *"Her infection has spread from her leg and is now in her whole blood system."*

CHAPTER TWENTY-ONE

THE SLEEPOVER

AUNT SARAH WAS HAPPY THAT NADJA had met another new friend. She always encouraged her to bring her friends to the house, and she loved going out to get all the extra goodies and treats for these sleepovers.

Nadja's only request was that Evron could stay the night. Aunt Sarah thought that was a wonderful idea as long as Matt would part with him. When Matthew heard the request, he laughingly said, "Well, okay, but only for one night."

Evron was happy as well. Nadja had told him a bit about Adi's problems and he suspected his thoughts and advice would probably be needed. This was certainly going to be more challenging than sleeping and chewing on doggie bones all weekend. Evron made one early suggestion to Nadja. "I think you and Aunt Sarah should offer to pick Adi up at her house."

"Oh, why is that?" replied Nadja. "Adi said her mom would drop her off here."

"I know," answered Evron, "but you said Adi was ashamed of her house so I think you should see it. It will give you a better idea of what she means."

"Maybe you're right, Evron. After all, I've seen a fair number of bad living conditions myself. I don't think I'll be too shocked."

Although Adi wasn't too happy about Nadja picking her up, she finally agreed. Adi and her mom were nervous as they waited for Nadja to arrive. As Nadja and Aunt Sarah drove up the winding driveway to Adi's small house, Aunt Sarah gasped, "Wow, the house does look a little run-down doesn't it? And it must be pretty cramped with four people living in it."

"I've seen worse," replied Nadja; "remember my crummy apartment building back home?"

"Yes, you're right, dear," continued Aunt Sarah, "and thankfully you don't have all those loud tenants yelling and screaming through thin walls around you anymore."

As they pulled up to the front door, Adi came out quickly with her mom and dad and her baby sister. She was carrying an overnight bag. Nadja introduced Adi to Aunt Sarah and then Adi introduced her parents. Everyone was a bit awkward at first, but, after a little idle chit chat, everyone felt more at ease. Before long, they had Adi's bag in the car and were heading for home.

Evron was waiting on the front porch as the car drove in the driveway. Nadja quickly introduced Adi to her furry friend. "Adi, this is Matthew's dog, Evron, and we're going to be looking after him for the night. He's going to be sleeping in our room."

"Oh cool," replied Adi; "I don't have a dog yet, but maybe someday. Hi, Evron," she continued, as she patted his head and scratched his ears.

Later the girls had Aunt Sarah's homemade pizza for dinner, along with "pink pop" as they called cream soda. To pass the evening, the girls played CD's, tried some video games, and even watched a movie. By eleven o'clock, Nadja had been waiting all night to bring up the topic of Adi's family situation. Finally she said, "I don't think your house looked that bad, Adi. You know you said you were so poor and all that."

"Oh, well it's pretty bad, Nadja. Look at how beautiful this house is!"

"Yeah, but if you could see where I lived before in my crummy apartment out West, you wouldn't think your home was that bad."

"Thanks for trying to make me feel better Nadja, but it's still not the same as living in this area."

"Well, I don't care where you live, Adi; you're still my new friend and I like you."

"Thanks, Nadja," Adi answered, grinning back.

Nadja was nervous now as she got ready to tell Adi her big secret. "Adi," she gulped, "I have a friend I want you to meet. I would like you to meet my talking dog friend, Evron."

Adi's mouth fell open as Evron said, "Hi Adi, it's nice to meet you. Nadja has told me a lot about you."

Nadja quickly continued, "Evron is a friend of mine and Matthew's. He has been a big help to me with all my problems; so, I thought he may be able to help you with yours."

Adi just stared at the talking Evron. "Omigosh," she gasped and she started to laugh. "Omigosh," she repeated again; and then, "Omigosh," one more time.

Nadja told Adi all about Evron's story. After she got accustomed to Evron's real identity, Adi felt really comfortable talking to him. "Geez, Evron," she said, "I haven't talked so much about my problems since I talked to Mr. Sobalsky." She continued, "My first big worry right now is my cat, Tippy. She's so sick and I don't know what to do."

Evron had an idea. "Nadja," he asked, "your Aunt Sarah used to work in a veterinarian's office, didn't she?"

"Yes, she was a veterinarian assistant."

"Well, let's ask her what she thinks about Tippy."

"Good idea," replied Nadja.

Aunt Sarah was excited when she was invited into her niece's bedroom on a "girls' weekend". She was glad to be able to help. She told Adi and Nadja that most veterinarians always have a special fund put aside for sick animals that are strays, victims of abuse, or from families with financial difficulties. At one time, she had worked for Dr. Cole in town and said she would be very happy to give him a call first thing in the morning. "Thanks for thinking about asking me for help, girls. I'm sure we'll work something out." Both girls smiled at Evron as she closed the door behind her. Evron winked back.

First thing Sunday morning, Aunt Sarah called Dr. Cole at his emergency number. He told her and the girls to bring Tippy in right away. The girls and Aunt Sarah drove in a rush to pick Tippy up. At the clinic, Dr. Cole gave Tippy a careful examination. "She sure is very sick," he said with a big frown. "Her infection has spread from her leg and is now in her whole blood system."

"She won't die will she, Dr. Cole?" Adi whispered, her lip quivering.

"No, she should be alright, Adi, but we'll have to keep her here and keep her on intravenous for a while."

"What's 'intravenous'?"

"Oh that's a tube that will supply her body with nutrients so that she can get her strength back. She's very weak now. I'm also going to put her on penicillin, a drug to fight her infection."

"Wow," replied Adi, looking really worried.

"And don't you worry about the cost, Adi; the clinic will take care of it. We're here to help."

"Oh, thank you so much, Dr. Cole; you've made me so happy. I've had Tippy all my life and she's such a friend to me."

"Pets are wonderful creatures, Adi," Dr. Cole continued. "I know just how you feel. That's why I became a veterinarian."

Adi continued, "I know they're not human Dr. Cole, but

A Time for Evron

because they're so dependent on us, I feel it's our responsibility to take care of them."

"You're right Adi. It's our job to look after them and protect them whenever we can."

Later that afternoon, back at the house, Adi picked up Evron and hugged him tightly. "Thanks Evron for helping me out. Even though you're not a normal dog like Earth's dogs, I still love you."

Evron and Nadja gave each other a big smile.

The next week, Adi received a letter at home with the veterinarian's return address on it. "Oh gosh" she said under her breath, "I hope it's not a big bill for Tippy."

Instead it was a personal letter from Dr. Cole addressed to her. It read:

> *"Dear Adi,*
> *I was most impressed last week with your caring and loving attitude, not only for your own cat, Tippy, but for all animals. To see such sensitivity and understanding in a person as young as yourself is truly outstanding. Despite your young age, I would be delighted to hire you part-time as an assistant in my practice.*
> *Dr. Wayne Cole"*

"Wowee!" screamed Adi as her mother ran into the room, wondering what was happening.

"That's wonderful news, honey," her mother exclaimed after reading the letter. "I'm very proud of you."

Adi started work the following weekend. Her job was for Saturdays from eight a.m. to four p.m. and she got paid five dollars an hour. "I'm so happy mom!" she exclaimed after her first day of work. "Now I can help our family with my small savings and I'm getting paid to be with the animals I love."

"Sure seems friendly enough," Mr. Burrows said as he
rubbed Buddy's neck and ears. *"I've got my last dog's collar
and leash. Let's see if Buddy likes them."*

CHAPTER TWENTY-TWO

A FEELING OF SELF-WORTH

WITHIN A FEW WEEKS, ADI'S BELOVED TIPPY was back home and gradually recovering. Adi was very happy.

She also had worked two Saturdays at Dr. Cole's office. It was exciting seeing all the different kinds of animals that people brought in. Some animals came just for their rabies shots and regular examinations, while others were very sick. A few had even died. She was heartbroken when this happened, not only for the animal, but for their owners as well. She understood the heartbreak these people were undergoing at losing their cherished pets.

At the same time, she learned about a darker side of human nature. Some animals that were brought in had been abused or abandoned. On a tip from a neighbor, one house in town was investigated and three dogs were found caged and barely alive. Their owner was away for days at a time and just left them without food or water. He was charged with animal neglect and abuse and was going to be taken to court.

In another case, a man brought in an old dog that he had supposedly found abandoned on a lonely country road. The dog had a broken leg. Dr. Cole suspected that this man was the real owner of the dog but he didn't want the expense of having the dog's leg repaired. The clinic would have to pay to heal the dog and then try to get him adopted. Adi was very sad each Saturday when she came to work and the dog was still there. His leg had healed, but no one wanted him. The clinic staff had even given him a name - Buddy. She thought Buddy seemed very depressed being in his cage all the time.

One day, on her way home from work, she suddenly thought of Mr. Burrows, Matt's elderly friend who lived nearby. She had been very impressed with Mr. Burrows's class presentation on World War II some months earlier.

She telephoned Matt as soon as she got home. "Matt," she said excitedly, "do you think Mr. Burrows would like a new dog to keep him company?"

"Gosh, I don't think so, Adi. He told me that after his last dog died, there would be no more dogs for him. He found he got too emotionally attached to them."

"Well, so he should," replied Adi. "They're wonderful friends."

"Oh I agree, Adi, but..."

"Matt," she interrupted, "please ask him if I can bring Buddy around sometime to meet him, just for a short visit. Dr. Cole said he would bring us over.

"Okay, I'll ask him, Adi, but don't get your hopes up."

"Thanks Matt, you're the best."

Within a half hour, Matt was at Mr. Burrows's door telling him about Adi's plan. Matt could hear himself trying to convince Mr. Burrows to adopt Buddy. "Adi says he is a wonderful dog, Mr. Burrows. He's completely house trained, isn't a furniture chewer, and loves going for walks."

"Oh, I don't know, Matt; dogs are a lot of work you know."

"Why not just meet him, Mr. Burrows? You don't have to say 'yes'."

"Well, it sure does get lonely around this big house at times, Matt." He paused, then said, "Okay, just a brief meeting this afternoon Matt. Will you be here?"

"For sure, Mr. Burrows; we'll be over in about an hour."

"Alright Matt, see you and Buddy then."

Matt could tell Mr. Burrows was a bit excited about the thought of another dog. Shortly afterwards, Adi, Dr. Cole, Matt and Buddy arrived at Mr. Burrows's house. "Hi again Mr. Burrows," Matt began, "this is my friend Adi, Dr. Cole and the star attraction, Buddy. Buddy wagged his tail furiously as Mr. Burrows bent down to take a closer look.

"Sure seems friendly enough," Mr. Burrows said as he rubbed Buddy's neck and ears. "I've got my last dog's collar and leash. Let's see if Buddy likes them." Matt and Adi and Dr. Cole held their breath as Mr. Burrows slipped the collar around Buddy's neck. How was he going to behave? Buddy sat quietly. "I think he's been well trained," Mr. Burrows said. "Look how obediently he's sitting. Now let's try the leash." He quickly clipped the leash to Buddy's new collar and began to walk away slowly. Buddy immediately got up and walked along with Mr. Burrows. He didn't tug or pull. "This is wonderful," smiled Mr. Burrows. "He's been very well trained; he's obviously been taught to heel. See how he stays by my leg when I walk and then sits when I stop."

'Oh, he's a great old dog, Mr. Burrows," Dr. Cole said as he grinned proudly.

"Guess what, guys?" Mr. Burrows asked mischievously. Everyone looked at him speechless...waiting. "I'm going to take him; I like him already. I just know we're going to get along."

Adi clapped her hands frantically, almost crying, she was so happy. Suddenly Mr. Burrows walked up to Adi. "And you, young lady, I want to thank you for thinking about me. It was very kind of you." He reached out and shook her hand. "Matthew has told me all about you and what you're doing for animals. Thank you so much."

Adi beamed from ear to ear.

"And another thing, Adi," Mr. Burrows continued, "I want to pay for Buddy's hospital stay."

"Oh that's not necessary," interrupted Dr. Cole.

"No, I insist, Dr. Cole. I can afford it. You can use that money to help someone else less fortunate."

Adi could barely contain her excitement.

"Oh, Mr. Burrows, thank you very much and I'm so happy for Buddy." She then leaned over and gave Buddy a big hug. "He's such a wonderful boy, Mr. Burrows; I'm sure you'll both be very happy."

"I know we will, Adi. I have just one request of you."

"Sure, Mr. Burrows."

"You must come and visit us both, whenever you can."

"I promise, Mr. Burrows; I promise."

On her way home with Dr. Cole and Matt, Adi said, "Thanks, Matt, for helping me out with Buddy and Mr. Burrows. It's sure nice to have friends like you."

"I'm happy it worked out, Adi, but you deserve most of the credit. You're the one who is always there for the animals."

"That's for sure," nodded Dr. Cole.

Except for schoolwork and her new friend Nadja, Adi discovered that most of her time was spent either at the clinic with the animals or daydreaming and worrying about them. One day, while she and Nadja were having lunch at school, she said, "You know, Nadja, how you organized the fund for families overseas in Azerbaijan?"

"Yes."

"Well, I think I'd like to organize some kind of an awareness program for disadvantaged animals right here in our own town."

"How would you do that?" inquired Nadja.

"Well, I know there is a canine control centre people can call for help with animals, but there really isn't a public awareness of how many poor, sick and homeless creatures there are."

"So what do you want to do?"

"I think I'll ask Mr. Sobalsky if I can convince our class to support me in an animal awareness fund drive. The students could canvass door to door in their neighborhoods. We could draw up our own pamphlets. Dr. Cole's clinic has some money set aside for homeless and abused animals, but he shouldn't have to provide all the money. It really should be a community responsibility."

"Wow," exclaimed Nadja, "you're really starting to sound like a young animal activist now!"

"Maybe so, but they need all the help they can get. They can't get it for themselves."

"Well, count me in," replied Nadja; "let me be your first volunteer." They both laughed out loud.

When Mr. Sobalsky heard of Adi's plan, he was proud that yet another of his students was starting a group to help others, this time defenseless animals. He also thought how far Adi had come from that tearful afternoon they had first spent together.

Within weeks, Adi had at least twenty active volunteers from her class. Dr. Cole's clinic paid for an advertisement in the local newspaper, appealing to the public to support the young students. Adi was even interviewed by the local newspaper, "The Tribune," and they also included her picture with one of the animals at the clinic.

During this time, her life became a frantic one as she continually had to be on the telephone, organizing volunteers or having meetings before and after school. Many details continually had to be worked out. Because she was the one in charge, most decisions rested with her. Although tired out at times, she loved her new responsibilities.

Within two months, her group had already raised over two hundred and fifty dollars. She was elated by the response. One day, after an afternoon meeting, she said to Nadja, "I'm so happy that everything is working out with the fund drive. You know I'm still upset about my home situation, but getting involved with this group has certainly made me feel better about myself. I don't have as much time to dwell on my own problems now."

"I agree, Adi," Nadja said as she put her arms around her. "It's a nice feeling to know you are helping to make life a bit easier for others."

One day, just as Adi's life seemed to be improving, it suddenly took a downturn. As she got off the school bus, her father was waiting for her at the door with her baby sister, Hannah, in his arms. He had a scowl on his face. "Now that you're home, do you think you might like to help me out around here for a change?"

"What ... what's wrong with you?" she asked carefully, sensing he was in a bad mood.

"I just think it would be nice if you could help out here for a change instead of always being in your own little fund-raising world."

"That's not fair," Adi yelled back, even though she regretted raising her voice with her father. "I do help out."

"Not as much anymore, now that you have all these other interests."

"Well, you're home all day and I'm not, you know!"

She felt badly again that she had spoken that way.

"It's not my fault, Adi," her father yelled at her. "It's not like I'm not trying to find a job."

"You're just jealous because I'm happier now and not caught up in the misery of this place."

Her father just looked at her as she ran off to the small bedroom that she shared with Hannah. She slammed the door. She was shaking as she fell onto her bed and cried into her pillow. Even when Hannah had been born a couple of years before, Adi still had felt she was her "daddy's little girl". She loved her mother, of course, but she and her father seemed to have a special bond. He always adored her. He used to say, "You're my special angel." That was one of his favorite phrases for her and he hummed a tune to go along with it.

"Why is this happening to me?" she quietly whispered to herself and her pillow. "Why does he always seem so unhappy with me now?"

Later that night, while her parents were watching television, she quietly smuggled the telephone into the closet and called Nadja. "Hi Nadja," she whispered.

"Hi Adi, what job have you got for me to do now?" Nadja teased.

"No job, Nadja; I'm really upset with my dad. We just had a big fight. Can I stay over this weekend?"

"Sure thing if you think it'll help."

"Thanks, I need some time away from him. And Nadja, can Evron come over too? I need to talk to him."

"Sure thing. I know Matthew won't mind."

Saturday night finally came and Adi couldn't wait to get to Nadja's. Her mother drove her over. Adi and her father hadn't spoken since the outburst earlier in the week. Her mother knew something was wrong between them, but so far she had said nothing.

"Now you have a great time tonight, dear," she said, as Adi got out of the car. "I think you need just to relax and forget about all your pressures."

"Thanks, Mom, I'll be okay." Adi knew her mother was hoping something would ease the tension that filled their house.

"Hi Nadja," she said as she bounded up the front steps. "Give me a hug quickly; I need to be hugged." As they embraced, she said, "there, I feel better already."

"C'mon into the kitchen and we'll start getting the pizza ready," Nadja said, as she helped Adi with her bag.

That evening after dinner, Evron and the three girls gathered in Nadja's room. Adi couldn't wait to get her frustrations out. "My dad is really starting to drive me crazy, Evron. I just don't know how to deal with him."

"How long has he been unemployed, Adi?" Evron asked.

"Just over two years. He was a supervisor for over twenty years at the local packing plant and then it suddenly closed down. Everyone that worked there lost his job."

"I assume he's tried finding other jobs."

"Oh, for sure, he really has tried very hard, but nothing seems available."

"Does he ever talk about it, Adi? Like how he feels about not finding a job?"

"He never says anything to me, Evron, but I hear my mom and him arguing sometimes about not having much money."

"What does he do all day with his spare time?" Evron asked.

"Oh, I guess he keeps the house clean and takes care of the baby. But not really much because there isn't a lot to do. It's not even our house; we're just renting."

"When he worked as a supervisor, how many people did he have under him?"

"Gosh, I think about twenty-five people. He was always very busy because he had a lot of responsibility. He even worked overtime to keep up."

Evron was quiet for a moment, then said, "Now think about this for a moment, Adi. There was your dad two years ago with all this responsibility and these people to take care of and then BANG, nothing: no job, no one to worry about, and worse still, no money coming in anymore. Now he's been living with these problems for two years."

"I know, Evron. I feel sorry for him, but what can I do?"

"I think the key right now is just trying to understand your father and how hard it must feel to be in his shoes."

Evron continued as both girls listened intently.

"Most people need some sense of accomplishment to make them feel good about themselves. Your dad's job and responsible position in the company would have made him feel good about himself and allowed him to provide a good living for all of you. Now you see he has none of that."

"You mean just like I feel so much better now that I'm involved in school with the animal fund?" asked Adi.

"Yes, the very same thing," replied Evron. "Unfortunately there are no easy answers for your dad."

"If only he could find something!," exclaimed Nadja.

"You know what?" said Evron excitedly. "Just last week, Matthew's dad was saying he thought he should probably hire an assistant manager to help him now that his business has grown so much. I wonder if..."

"Do you think maybe my dad could be his assistant manager?" Adi enthused.

"Well, maybe, Adi," continued Evron, "just maybe. Obviously your father has managerial skills if he had twenty-five people working under him."

"For sure," she replied excitedly. "I'll speak to Matthew tomorrow and we'll all keep our fingers crossed." Then they all laughed and held up their crossed fingers and paws in front of each other.

Later that week, Matthew did speak to his father about Adi's dad and his situation.

"Adi's father might be a good assistant for me," his father replied. "I'd prefer to have someone with a good work record who is known in the community. I've always heard great things about him. I'll give him a call after dinner; he might just be the right one."

"Just one request please, Dad?" continued Matthew.

"What's that?"

"Don't tell him any of the kids were involved. We feel it's better if he thought it was strictly your idea. You know how adults are and all."

"No problem Matt, I agree. I'll just say he was recommended by a customer."

Matt's dad did call Adi's father and set up an interview. Both men got along well and had many interests in common, including their children. Adi's father was hired, became a good assistant manager, and helped business to blossom at the service centre.

One day, much later at school, Matt, Nadja and Adi were having lunch together and Matt said, "You know, Adi, my dad and I sure like your father; he's a great guy and dad says he's a terrific assistant."

"Thanks, Matt," she replied. "Things are so much better at home. He's a lot happier now that he has a job again. We're all much happier."

"That's great, Adi. There's also a bonus in this for me as well. Guess what it is?"

"Tell us, Matt," begged Nadja.

"Now I get to see my dad much more often because he doesn't have to spend so many hours working at the station."

"So you're happier too," continued Adi.

"For sure" replied Matt, smiling. "I guess this is what you call a 'win-win' situation."

A Time for Evron

*The snowmobile lurched forward towards the middle of the river.
Suddenly, Evron appeared running along the side.*

CHAPTER TWENTY-THREE

SPECIAL POWER

BY LATE FEBRUARY, THE WEATHER had really turned cold and the snow was beginning to pile up on the ground. Mr. and Mrs. Ross, Matt's young neighbors down the street, had just bought twin snowmobiles with their own special matching trailer. Mr. Ross had proudly shown Matt the new machines; he was excited that he and Mrs. Ross were going to have a snowmobiling weekend soon. Matt thought that he seemed just like a little boy; he was so excited. Matt hoped that someday this winter, Mr. Ross would offer to take him and Richard for a ride.

That Friday afternoon, school was dismissed early because a frozen watermain broke, cutting the water supply off. Richard and Matt were delighted, and eager to get home early to play some new video games. Just as they were rounding the corner to Matt's house, they were shocked to see two men push Mr. Ross's new snowmobile trailer onto the road and attach it behind their van.

"Look at that!" whispered Matt, as he grabbed Richard's arm.

"What's wrong?"

"Shhh," continued Matt, "look at those guys over there; I think they're stealing Mr. Ross's snowmobiles."

"Maybe they have permission to take them," replied Richard.

"No way," said Matt. "Mr. and Mrs. Ross are going away tonight for a snowmobile weekend. He's as excited about it as a kid."

"Okay, so what do you want to do about it?"

"I ... I don't know. Let's sneak up closer."

By darting behind trees and hedges, the boys were finally beside Mr. Ross's garage. They kept looking for someone else around to help them, but the neighborhood seemed deserted.

They were now close enough to hear the men talking. "Okay Max, we're ready to get these off to the warehouse. This will make twenty machines we've taken now. It's been a good week's work. We're going to make great money on the black market."

Both boys looked at each other with mouths agape.

"You were right!" gasped Richard.

"Shhh," whispered Matt, as he put his fingers to his lips.

"What now?" whispered Richard.

"I don't see any license plate on that van," continued Matt.

Just then the van and trailer started to drive slowly away. "Quick!" said Matt, as he pulled at Richard's coat sleeve. "Lets jump inside the hood of the trailer."

The gleaming new trailer had a custom made hood which curved up from the front and partly over the snowmobiles, to protect them from dirt and water while they were being towed. Matt and Richard easily jumped onto the trailer and scrambled under the hood. They held tightly onto the snowmobiles.

"Now what are we going to do?" asked Richard fearfully.

"We'll find out where they're going with these and then we can call the police."

"How are we going to do that?" asked Richard. "What if we can't find a telephone? Oh Matthew, I wish we were home playing video games!"

The boys hung on tightly as the van sped down side streets, rounded corners sharply, and dodged in and out around slow moving cars. Obviously the thieves wanted to get somewhere in a hurry. Then, the boys peered out from under the hood and they started to recognize the area through which they were traveling. They were heading down to the river near where they had gone fishing last fall.

Suddenly the trailer lurched to a halt, and turned quickly into a driveway. The whole area looked completely different with all the snow, but they could still see the river in the distance. Suddenly a huge set of doors opened in front of them and they entered an old warehouse. The boys stared around in awe at more than a hundred gleaming snowmobiles. They crouched together closely under the trailer's hood as the huge warehouse doors slammed shut. They could hear voices.

"Let's get a coffee, Willy; then we'll unload these beauties," said one of the thieves.

The boys breathed quietly as they heard the footsteps move away. Richard peeked around the corner and saw the men enter an old office. "Now, where's this t-t-telephone you talked about Smarty?" he stuttered to Matt. "And even if we could call the police, do you know where we are exactly? They'll never find us in here."

"Don't worry," replied Matt. "Evron will find us."

"Are you kidding me?" cried Richard. "He can't find us here."

"Yes he can; we have a special code. If I say it out loud, he knows I'm in trouble. I'm never to use it unless there's a serious emergency."

"Well, I'd sure say this is a serious emergency," replied Richard, sarcastically. "Have you ever tried this code out together?"

"Well, no; I've never been in trouble before."

"Oh wonderful Matt; this is just dandy. Now we're going to try a code you've never even tried before!"

Just then the trailer tipped backward and both boys tumbled out onto the floor as the thieves returned from the office. "Oh boy, Boss, look what we have here," gasped one of the thieves as he grabbed each boy with his powerful arms.

"Well, well, two stowaways I see," replied the big burly leader.

"You're robbers!" yelled Matt. "You stole my neighbor's snowmobiles. We're going to call the police."

"I don't think so," replied the cruel looking thief.

"What are we going to do with them?" asked his assistant. "They've seen everything. They even know what we look like."

"I know. It's tough but we can't risk leaving them around. They'll have to have an accident."

"What do you mean, Boss?"

"Well, the river still isn't completely frozen in the middle. Suppose these boys were joyriding on a snowmobile on the icy river and accidentally hit a water spot. I guess they'd sink and drown."

Richard and Matt stared at each other in terror.

"C'mon boys, let's get one of these nice new snowmobiles out on the ice for you. We're going to send you on a joyride right out to the middle of the river where that nice cold, deep water is waiting just for you."

"We'll jump!" screamed Richard.

"Oh no, you won't. We're going to tie you together to the machine with some special tape. It will come off when you hit the water. Don't worry, you'll drown quickly."

The boys were breathing quickly now.

"Red apples have an orangey taste ... Red apples have an orangey taste ... Red apples have an orangey taste!!" Matt repeated out loud.

Richard looked at him in disbelief. The thieves stared as well.

"What's wrong with the kid, Boss?"

"I think he's lost his marbles!" the other replied.

Both broke out in laughter and began tying the boys to one

of the snowmobiles; then, the thieves dragged the snowmobile outside onto the snow. They started it up and slowly headed onto the frozen river's edge with both boys tied to the seat.

"It won't be long now boys; it'll soon be time for a nice refreshing cold swim," mocked one of them.

"See that nice watery patch out there? Well, we'll just jam this throttle down and head you two toward it."

Suddenly there was a loud sound.

"Halt, don't move!"

Both thieves turned abruptly to see two police officers running toward them. They released the machine and, with the tape holding it in full throttle, the snowmobile lurched forward towards the middle of the river. Suddenly, Evron appeared running along the side. He jumped onto the handlebars and tore the tape from the throttle bar. The machine stopped abruptly only meters from the open water. Then he tore more tape from the boys' hands and feet.

He jumped into their arms; both boys were sobbing as they hugged and kissed him.

"Oh Evron! " cried Matt, "I wasn't sure our code would work."

"It always works," replied Evron. "Always."

The boys and Evron returned to the shoreline where the two police officers were handcuffing the thieves and putting them into the cruiser. "Are you boys alright?" yelled one of the officers.

"We're fine thanks," replied Matt, "just a bit scared."

"These men are part of a big crime ring we've been trying to break for months. Is that your dog, young man?" the officer continued.

"Yes it is, officer."

"Well, you're both lucky that we happened to be chasing him into this area!"

"How's that?" replied Richard.

"This dog came into our precinct office about ten minutes ago and grabbed two reports from our desk. We were chasing him in the cruiser when we luckily ended up here."

"Wow," replied Matt, "we really are lucky."

"If I didn't know better," continued the officer, "I would almost think that the dog had planned it, that he deliberately led us here."

"That would be funny, wouldn't it?" chuckled Richard.

Both boys and Evron got a ride home in the second police cruiser. After thanking the officer for the ride, they headed for Matt's kitchen and some cookies and juice. Nobody talked for a few minutes, then Richard said, "Okay, Evron and Matthew, just what went on back there? What is this 'Red apples have an orangey taste'?"

Evron and Matt looked at each other and smiled.

"That's the special code I told you about earlier,"

"What you heard Matthew say," continued Evron, "is really a code between us. The code is to be used only when he is in serious trouble. This, of course, was a good example of that."

"Why such a silly phrase?" asked Richard.

"The phrase is silly so that if it is overheard, as it was today, no one would understand it's meaning. If Matt had blurted out, 'Help us, Evron; call the police', he could have alerted the thieves early. They might have escaped, and you two could have drowned. Because he used silly phrases, they just ignored him."

"How did you guys come up with that code?"

"Well," continued Evron, "the idea is to have a sentence relating to nature that really makes no sense. 'Red apples taste like oranges' is silly and makes no sense does it?"

"I get it," laughed Richard. "So, I could say, 'Pigs fly south for the winter' or 'Roses grow in my flower bed in winter'."

"Exactly," smiled Matt.

A Time for Evron

"Really then, Evron, you're just like a guardian angel for Matthew."

"I guess in a way you could say that, but I help others too, as you already know, Richard."

"So, now can I get my own dog, with my own code?"

"I'm working on it Richard," Evron replied. "That's why there are some of us here now on Earth, seeing how we can bring it about."

"I hope it's soon, Evron. Can I be one of the first kids to get a dog if more come?"

"For sure, Richard, I promise," Evron replied as he gave him a lick on the cheek.

Matt and Richard then went into Matt's bedroom to play the new video games. The games seemed pretty boring, however, after the snowmobile escapade.

*The boys were showing off by darting in
and out around the girls.*

CHAPTER TWENTY-FOUR

HURTING OTHERS

SPRING FINALLY ARRIVED sometime in late April. The boys loved the change in the weather, especially because they could finally get out their skateboards without worrying about snow or slush. Many of the girls seemed to prefer rollerblading. The neighborhood was a busy place on nice Saturday afternoons with skateboards and rollerblades speeding around each other every which way.

A favorite spot to take a break and have a drink was Marty's Variety Store. Because it was getting so warm, Marty already had picnic tables and umbrellas out. It was fun to sit at a table in the warm sun, chat with your friends and watch the world go by.

On this particular day, Richard and Matt saw Nadja and her new friend, Michelle, sitting at a table as they zoomed up on their boards. Michelle's father had died the year before of cancer and the girls met at a bereavement group.

"Hi Michelle, hi Nadja!" the boys chimed.

"Hi guys!" the girls replied. Even though Matt and Nadja were only good friends now, he still couldn't get rid of that special feeling he had for her. Every time he was near her, he was sure his heart beat differently. He was sure it was just his hopeful imagination, but at times he thought she still looked at him in that special way as well.

"So what are you guys going to do today?" asked Michelle.

"Oh, we're just out getting some board practice," Richard replied.

"We may build a ramp and try some new jumps," added Matt. "How about you girls?"

"I just had a sleepover at Michelle's last night so we're rollerblading back to my house."

"Well, why don't we skateboard along with you?" answered Matt.

"Sure, sounds like fun!"

The girls cleaned up their table and soon the four of them were off down the street. The boys were showing off by darting in and out around the girls. At one point, Matt grabbed Nadja's hand and spun her around. She laughed hysterically; he loved making her laugh.

After dinner that evening, Nadja telephoned Matt. "Hi Matthew, it's Nadja."

"I'd know that voice anywhere," joked Matt.

"I wonder if I can come over and speak to you for a few minutes?"

"Sure thing," he replied. He wasn't sure what she wanted, but the fact that she had called him about anything made him very happy.

Matthew came out to meet her on the front porch. It was warm enough for them to sit on the new settee. Evron lay near-by. Nadja began, "I couldn't speak to you earlier in front of Richard and Michelle, but I'm upset about her and I need to talk to you and Evron about it."

"Go ahead," answered Matt.

"Well, I told you I had a sleepover at Michelle's last night. Her mom has gone away for the weekend and her older brother, Daryl, is responsible for her. He's seventeen, so there's really no problem.

A Time for Evron

Even Aunt Sarah thought everything was alright. Daryl isn't allowed to leave Michelle alone; so he usually has his friend Michael over and they watch T.V. or play basketball in the driveway."

Matt and Evron listened as Nadja continued. "Anyway, Michelle and I were ready to go to sleep about one a.m. and we turned the lights out and were still talking in bed. We stopped talking for awhile and I thought she'd gone to sleep. Then she said, 'I guess Daryl and Michael aren't coming to my room tonight because you're here.' "

"I said, 'What do you mean, come to your room'?"

"Then she said, 'Promise you won't tell anyone if I tell you.' "

"I said, 'Sure, I promise.' "

"Michelle continued, 'Sometimes they come at night and undress me. They take my pajamas off and look at me.' "

" 'They what?' I said in disbelief.' "

" 'They take all my clothes off. Then ... then they touch me.' "

"'Where?' I screamed."

" 'Down there', she replied."

" 'What else do they do?' "

" 'Nothing, they just laugh and giggle; then they leave.' "

" 'Why do you let them do it?' I asked"

" 'I don't want to, but Daryl says I'll get in big trouble with Mom if I squeal on them. He says there's nothing really wrong with what they're doing and that Mom won't believe me anyway. So I'm scared to say anything.' "

Matt and Evron sat in stunned silence as Nadja told her story. She continued, "I'm so sorry I broke my promise to Michelle not to tell anyone, but I just had to. I trust you both so much. Do you think this is 'no big deal', as her brother says?"

"Absolutely not," replied Matthew; "it's sick."

Then Evron spoke very seriously. "Matt's right of course, Nadja; it is sick. Do you think Michelle would talk to you and me alone?"

"What about me too?" asked Matt.

"No, I don't think so, Matt. You're a boy and there's no need for Michelle to know that anyone else knows but me. She'll be very sensitive about this. Do you understand what I mean, Matthew?"

"Yes, I think you're right, Evron."

"And of course, Matthew, you realize that what Nadja has told you is strictly confidential. You must repeat it to no one."

"Of course not," he replied.

"What do we do now, Evron?" asked Nadja.

"Well," he sighed, "I guess someone else is going to discover who I really am!"

"You don't mind that?"

"Not at all. The first thing we should do, Nadja, is to sit down privately with Michelle."

"Great! I'll have her over after school on Monday and you can be with us."

"That sounds good," winked Evron.

Nadja could hardly wait for Monday to come so that she could start to help her troubled friend. Michelle had no idea what Nadja had planned for her. After arriving home from school that day, Michelle and Nadja were sitting quietly in the late afternoon sun. Nadja broke the silence.

"Michelle, I have a friend who has helped me a lot with my family problems. He is very wise and has always been there for me in difficult times. I'd like you to meet Evron."

"Hi Michelle," Evron said gently. "It's nice to meet you."

Michelle started laughing. "You're playing a trick on me aren't you, Nadja?"

"No, honestly, he's for real!"

Nadja then proceeded to tell Michelle Evron's story.

"It's still so hard to believe," she added.

A Time for Evron

"The reason Evron is here today, Michelle, is that ... I hope you'll forgive me ... I told him about your brother and his friend. He wants to help."

"Why did you tell, Nadja? You promised you wouldn't!"

"I had to, Michelle. I don't want you to continue being hurt."

"She's right, Michelle; you must not continue like this. It has to stop," added Evron.

"How will I stop it, Evron? He'll get me in trouble if I squeal on him."

"No such thing is going to happen," he replied. "This is what I would like you to do. Will you trust me?"

"If Nadja believes in you, then I'll try, Evron."

"Good! Please listen carefully. The first thing you do is this ... sit down with Daryl and tell him that if he ever touches you again or comes near you as he has before, you'll tell your mother everything. If he comes near you when she isn't around, tell him you'll call 911. Make it clear that he can be charged with sexual assault and end up in police custody."

"But he says I'm overreacting to the situation, Evron."

"Nonsense, this is a very, very serious thing he's doing. No one is allowed to touch another person without his or her permission, especially in places that are normally covered with clothing."

"What about holding a friend's hand or kissing your parents, or kissing my girlfriends on the cheek?"

"That isn't the same thing at all, Michelle. That isn't touching in a sexual manner. Touching sexual organs and other covered body parts is simply out of the question. You shouldn't even have to worry about it."

"What if he laughs me off and ignores me?"

"Then you go to your mom immediately."

"What if she gets really upset with him?"

"That's too bad," replied Evron. "This isn't your fault; it's his. You're an innocent victim."

Michelle sat quietly for a moment, obviously in deep thought. "I'm miserable always worrying about him coming near me. I guess I can't be any more miserable if she finds out."

"No, you'll be far less miserable, Michelle. You'll be able to live peacefully every day, without being scared."

"I feel better already now that you know. I'm sorry I got mad at you, Nadja. Thanks for caring about me so much."

Nadja and Michelle had tears in their eyes as they hugged each other.

"You see, girls, this kind of hugging is okay," Evron remarked, trying to lighten up the situation.

The next night, Michelle and her brother Daryl had their talk. He seemed scared by her threat to tell everything, and promised he would never do those things again. "Do you think you can ever forgive me, Michelle?" he asked.

"I don't know," she replied. "Only time will tell."

"I'm still your brother; don't forget," he pleaded.

Michelle looked at Daryl blankly and answered sadly, "I used to look up to you, Daryl, and was proud to have you as my older brother. I'm not sure I'll ever feel that way about you again."

In the weeks and months to come, Daryl was true to his word and Michelle never had to worry about him anymore. She was sad at times though, because, even though he was her brother, she didn't particularly like him anymore.

A Time for Evron

*One time, as Nadja came shivering out of the pool, Matthew held
out her big beach towel for her and wrapped it around her.*

CHAPTER TWENTY-FIVE

MORE THAN JUST A FRIEND

AS THE WARM SPRING DAYS finally turned into the heat of summer, Matthew was happy with his favorite season. He loved running outside in the mornings without his sweater or jacket on and it was pure joy to pick up the morning paper in his bare feet. He loved having no storm doors or windows to shut and the feeling of a warm summer breeze coming through his bedroom window at night.

Nadja's aunt and uncle had a swimming pool and Matt was frequently invited over to swim, now that they had a young person living in their house again. He always loved diving and now he was teaching Nadja some complicated back flips and twists. Often she had several of her classmates over together, but at other times there was just Matthew. He was sure they were becoming closer again. He loved to lay his towel out on the ground by the pool and dry himself in the hot sun; Nadja often lay her towel beside his. One of their favorite games was to look up at the sky together and try to imagine faces or images formed by the passing clouds. Aunt Sarah regularly heard Nadja laughing with Matthew and she really hoped that her adopted daughter was feeling happy and accepted in her new home.

One time, as Nadja came shivering out of the pool, Matthew

held out her big beach towel for her and wrapped it around her. Without really thinking about it, he continued to keep his arms around her too. She lay her head on his shoulder. He held her like this for what seemed forever and then kissed her softly. She smiled back at him, then asked playfully, "Hi, who are you?"

"Oh just some guy with a crush on you," he answered in a whisper.

She gave him a quick kiss back. Just then Aunt Sarah said, "Nadja, it's time for dinner." Nadja and Matt weren't sure whether she did this deliberately or not, but it really was time for him to go.

They both tried not to see each other too much, but they did go out to the movies sometimes, and at other times, took long walks and bike rides together. By the beginning of June, they wouldn't let their friends say they were going steady or anything like that, but they were certainly more than just friends.

A Time for Evron

"I don't mind sharing you," Nadja laughed during
one dance with Matthew, *"but not quite as much tonight
as I would have normally."*

CHAPTER TWENTY-SIX

MOVING ON

ONE DAY, AFTER MATT ARRIVED HOME from school and was preparing his dad's dinner, Evron came in and sat down beside him.

"If you've got a few minutes before you take dinner to your dad at the station, I'd like to talk to you," he said quietly.

"Sure, Evron. You sound so serious; what's up?"

"I've been in contact with my other friends around Earth, Matthew, and it's time for us to go back to our own galaxy for a while."

"Oh, no," cried Matthew.

"It won't be forever, Matthew, and besides I have a proposal for you."

"What's that, Evron?"

"We would like to take our Earth friends with us, Matt. We want all of you to come with us for a while. There are twelve of you young earthlings from around the planet. Our hope is to take all of you back and learn from your group."

"What do you want to learn?"

"Well, for one thing, you all come from different countries. We want to study your similarities and differences. We want to see how you all interact and live with each other for awhile. We want to hear various ideas about such things as the environment and world peace and what social issues are important to you. Think about what you've learned from your experience with Vahid."

"Wow!! For sure," replied Matt. Then he was silent for a moment, deep in thought. "You mean sort of like all of us going away to camp together," he finally gasped.

Evron laughed, "I never thought of it like that, but that's a good way to put it – a trip to a far away camp."

"What will our parents say?" asked Matt.

"Well, obviously your dad will have to know about me and give his permission, as well as all the other parents involved."

"How do you think they'll react?"

"I'm hoping, Matt, that they will realize we're working toward a better understanding and communication between all the people on Earth, and that your generation is the one which can really make a difference. It's important that you young people start working on it now; I'm guessing that they'll go for it."

"Well, I'm sure in favor of it," gulped Matt.

Evron and his team worked quickly with all the parents. Special meetings were held and specific details of the mission were outlined. All the adults gladly gave their permission. They were proud that their kids had been chosen for such an important adventure. It was decided to tell everyone in the communities concerned that their particular young people were going away to attend a private school out of the country for awhile. "This isn't a lie," Evron chuckled; "it sure is out of the country."

It wasn't certain how long the kids would be away, but probably for half a year or more. At Matthew's school, only Nadja and Richard were to know. Matthew and Evron decided to tell them together. Richard held back his tears and tried to make a joke. "Are you sure you don't have room for me too, old buddy?"

Nadja was crying quietly as she hugged Matt. She wouldn't let go. "I'm going to miss you so much," she whispered to him.

"I'll miss you too," he whispered back.

Then she asked, "Are you still going to take me to the year end dance?"

"For sure!" he smiled back. "We leave the week afterwards."

The Year End School Dance was beautiful. The auditorium was decorated with dazzling ribbons and hundreds and hundreds of fresh flowers. Nadja was one of the student organizers and the one thing she wanted more than anything else was one of those big mirrored balls that rotated from the ceiling. When the colored lights reflected off it, it shone thousands of moving light rays all around the room. "Very romantic to dance to," she said.

Although she had been excited about the dance for weeks, she was upset about it too. She knew it would be one of the last times she would be able to spend with Matt for a long time.

The big night finally arrived. The girls all looked beautiful in their dresses and the boys were charming in their shirts and ties. Some even wore suits and tuxedos.

Not everyone took 'dates' to the dance and it was common for all the students to trade around partners for dances. "I don't mind sharing you," Nadja laughed during one dance with Matthew, "but not quite as much tonight, as I would have normally."

He hugged her and said, "Guess what?"

"Tell me," she replied excitedly.

"I've requested a special song to be played that's from me to you."

"You're kidding!"

"No, I hope you don't think it's too mushy. It's coming up next."

"What's it called?"

"This I Promise You," he whispered in her ear as he put his arms around her. Nadja loved the words and, as they slowly danced, she wondered if she had ever been happier.

Time flew by over the next little while and the departure day finally arrived. Evron and Matthew checked over his suitcases and last minute details. Matt's dad got ready to drive Nadja, Richard, Matt and Evron out to a secluded country field just after dark. It was there that Evron's spaceship would arrive to pick up Matt and himself.

Nadja was tense as she and Richard got into the car. Nobody spoke much during the drive. The sky was moonlit with thousands of stars and Nadja thought that, under different circumstances, it could have even been a very romantic evening.

The car finally pulled to a stop and they all got out. Matt's dad got his two suitcases from the trunk while Nadja held Matt's hand tightly.

"I think you're going to crush my knuckles," he whispered to her.

"Too bad," she responded.

"There it is," said Evron quietly as he pointed off in the distance.

The spot was only a flickering speck at first. Suddenly, it became much larger and, in a very short time, was hovering over them. Everyone was in awe at the spectacle of the huge multicolored disc with lights flashing everywhere. The surprising thing was that there was hardly any noise - just a soft whirring sound.

As the huge spaceship descended, a large door opened and a set of steps lowered to the field. Evron looked at Matthew. "It's time, Matthew," he said.

Matthew had tears in his eyes as he ran into his dad's arms. His dad had tears too. Nadja, crying, grabbed Richard as he tried to comfort her. Matthew moved around to hug everyone. Nadja was last. He held her so closely, he was afraid he was going to crush her. "Bye for now," he whispered to her as he kissed her softly. "I love you."

"I love you too," she whispered back.

A Time for Evron

He and Evron climbed the steps together, each holding a suitcase. As they got to the top, they turned around and waved. Everybody on the ground waved back, as they tried to force smiles.

Slowly the steps receded into the gaping hole, and the ship's huge doors quietly shut tightly. The massive machine slowly lifted away from the field and then quickly darted upward. Within a minute, it was only a speck of light again. It looked like just another star in the universe.

AUTHOR'S LETTER

Dear Young Reader,

As a teacher and counselor, I am part of a group of professional people working with you to achieve your long-term goals. Whether by encouraging you to develop intellectually, or by supporting you in the search for self-fulfillment, we always try to be there for you. In this capacity, we are constantly searching for new ideas to stimulate you.

Recently, while attending a conference, I discovered the following excerpt which was part of the programme for the Grade 8 graduation exercises of The Network of Sacred Heart Schools in Chicago:

"Helped by adults and peers to be
truthful and honest with yourself,
you will grow in self-confidence
by dealing realistically
with your gifts and limitations.
Not all are leaders,
not all are athletes,
not all are artists.
Do not grieve what talents God did not give you,
but recognize and rejoice in
the worth of others.
Discover your particular gifts
and develop your unique potential.
If you are sensitive to people, care for them.
If you are a scholar, share your love of learning.
If you can create with your hands, give the world beauty.
When you find humor and laughter in your life, give
others your joy.
The gift you have received, give as a gift." *

I find these words to be truly inspiring. Along with the lyrics of the song, *"BELIEVE IN YOU"*, quoted at the beginning of my book, they remind me of our individual sensitivity and our need, not only to seek help, but also to offer help to others. My wish is that these words may also inspire each of you, at whatever stage you are, in your personal growth.

As an adult interacting with young people like yourselves, I never cease to be amazed by your sincerity, innocence, sense of humor, need for belonging and approval, as well as the trust you put in me. It is indeed a privilege to be an ongoing part of your world.

My hope for each of you is the very best that life may bring your way.

*reprinted by permission from *"Life at the Sacred Heart"*, the Network of Sacred Heart Schools, e-mail address nshoffice@sofie.org

Bryan Smillie is a graduate of the University of Western Ontario and the University of Toronto. He is a recently retired teacher and counselor with over thirty years experience working with young people from kindergarten to pre-college and university. He continues to teach and counsel part-time at both the elementary and secondary school levels. He also has his own counseling practice and has counseled part-time at ***Kids Help Phone***, a confidential counseling and referral service for kids across Canada. He lives with his family near Toronto, Ontario.

Mike Rooth is a graduate of Sheridan College's Interpretive Illustration program. A St. Catherines native, he now resides in Oakville, Ontario where he works as a freelance illustrator. Over the past two years, his work has appeared in a wide variety of publications, local and international; this is his first solo venture into the world of children's publishing.